heretofore

a novel

Todd Crawshaw

CrowsnestPublishing.com

Visit: www.toddcrawshaw.com

ISBN-10: 0615586155
ISBN-13: 978-0-615-58615-1

Book design & illustrations: Todd Crawshaw
Editorial Consultant: Robyn Russell
Back cover photo: Michael Mustacchi

CrowsnestPublishing.com

Printed in the United States of America

ALSO BY TODD CRAWSHAW

Light-Years in the Dark
storypoems

Exploits of the Satyr
a novel

contents

– chapter one –
Wyatt T. Frog 1

– chapter two –
Riley Crow 25

– chapter three –
Izzy Beaver 35

– chapter four –
Hazel Squirrel 51

– chapter five –
Harold Hare 69

– chapter six –
Wick Weasel 85

– chapter seven –
Scarlet Fox 103

– chapter eight –
Camille Chameleon 119

– chapter nine –
Owen Owl 141

– chapter ten –
Zhena Spider 175

– chapter eleven –
Angelo Iguana 197

– chapter twelve –
Prater Mantis 219

Curiosity

killed the cat.

Satisfaction

brought it back.

— a proverb

chapter one

Wyatt T. Frog

Wyatt T. Frog had observed many fascinating things in his life but never had he seen a girl falling from the sky—until now. As an artist, Wyatt was a keen observer. Apples, pine cones, branches, even squirrels fell from the sky. Squirrels like Hazel who had fallen from a tree one day to land with a thump in the grass and startle him. She was the cutest rodent he had ever seen. Her chestnut fur had mesmerized him, along with her fluffy tail and her brown eyes rolled backwards, beautiful even when unconscious. On impulse, Wyatt decided he would rescue her. He dragged her by the tail, circumnavigating the tall tufts of crab grass until he reached his beachfront house that overlooked a river, where he continued to pull her by the tail over his decorative path of river rocks, then up and over three steps, landing her on the porch, before tugging her across the threshold, a doorway made from ornamental reeds, next sliding her like a mop over floorboards made of driftwood smoothed by sand-and-surf, finally rolling her body onto his luxurious bed of moss. After covering her with a downy quilt, he started a fire in the hearth. He then sat beside her, keeping her warm, admiring her until she awoke. With a shriek. She clenched the quilt to her chest and slapped his face. He was now madly in love with her. Yes, things fell from the sky. But never little girls.

What Wyatt first saw in the sky had been a flickering speck in his peripheral vision before turning his head to glimpse what he believed to be somebody draped in a flapping red pinafore with long black hair trailing vertically in the air like the tail of a plummeting kite. Whatever he had seen had struck the meadow with an audible thud. Landing only a hop-skip-and-jump away. So Wyatt hopped over to investigate. He now found himself looking down upon this little girl. And little she was—very little. Not only in age, but in size. She was no bigger than a frog. Which Wyatt knew something about, being a frog himself.

The morning had begun so peacefully. A glorious sun wavering upwards on its journey across the sky, its yellow warmth in perfect harmony with a meandering cool blue breeze teasing the long stems of sparkling green grass. Wyatt had come prepared to paint, but was so enthralled by the delightful day he decided not to apply a single brushstroke of color. He returned his instruments of creation back into their wooden box and allowed the canvas to stay raised like a white flag upon its easel, where it remained blank. Surrendering to nature's beauty. Willingly admitting defeat, he had tamped the grass to cushion the ground upon which he reclined, then gazed languidly into the sky with a rebellious notion to do nothing at all – simply enjoy himself.

Which was what he *had* been doing before this little girl dropped from the sky to disrupt his quietude.

Wyatt had never been this close to a human before. Discounting, of course, his vivid nightmare of being captured by a gigantic boy who toyed with him mercilessly. Imprisoned inside a cave of pink flesh, a blunt yellow fingernail poking him, and a foul wind blowing in his face, Wyatt had soiled himself. A godlike voice had intervened on his behalf, which prompted his captor to release and drop him. Wyatt's heart was thumping wildly all over again from the memory. He removed his black beret and fanned his face. He loosened his red cravat and opened the collar of his black velvet jacket for air. He wore these articles of clothing in honor of Delacroix, his idol, the French romantic painter whose dramatic style – artwork depicting moments of extreme passion – had offended the academic hierarchy. Wyatt was on a quest himself to offend and shake up the rigid mores of the established view. He knew enough to know he was on a quest. What that quest entailed he wasn't sure, only that he was passionate about it. So he painted passionately – well, on most days – to attain success. At least some measure of success. To rise in stature. Yet, despite all his efforts—alas, he remained small. A frog.

Wyatt's concave forehead creased in thought. He refused to let the mishaps in life or his genetic deficiencies make him bitter and ruin a perfectly good day. Trials and tribulations forced one to make the most of what they had, as Delacroix had. Everyone had flaws. The purpose for existing, Wyatt philosophized, was to rise and shine above this earthly muck – not whine.

Wyatt sucked in air to meditate upon this notion.

He closed the large lids of his red protruding eyes in an attempt to summon the guiding spirit of Delacroix. Who sometimes made guest appearances when it was convenient. Though never certain of this, he sensed it, certainly wishing it were true. Compelled to check, Wyatt peeked but only saw stalks of grass swaying in the wind.

He massaged a spot between his eyes and muttered to himself, "This little girl could be an *illusion*. A specter of the mind, conjured by spontaneous combustion of disparate parts reassembled anew, as with all works of art." He touched his thin lips with a nubby fingertip and smiled, liking the construct of his words. His next remark was voiced loudly at his critics who gave him worse than bad reviews – they ignored him. He turned upon the blades of grass to scold and edify them by quoting Delacroix: "I spoil each picture – just a little – in order to perfect it!"

Wyatt composed himself, reinvigorated. He tightened his cravat and picked at flecks of dried oil paint which adorned his jacket and pants, before splaying his red fingers to admire their artistic length and expansive nubs. The crowning touch was his beret. He tilted it rakishly in a proactive manner. First impressions were important. This little girl was liable to wake at any moment. He was prepared to impress her. But her eyes refused to open. Mildly miffed, Wyatt nudged the pink skin of her arm with the toe of his sandaled foot to help determine what it was he was dealing with.

"Humm," he mused, "she certainly *feels* real."

Wondering what he should do, Wyatt sought help from the sky.

He noticed how it resembled a watercolor, a beautiful wash of *bleu celeste* streaked through the middle by a diffused evergreen cloud, as if to foreshadow a hazy elongated apparition – the branch of a tree. Wyatt's imagination was stirred with the genesis for a new painting. A vision depicting the magical realm and dwelling place of fairies and sprightly little girls who fell from the sky.

His reverie dispersed upon hearing a voice:

"Who *are* you?"

Wyatt realized the little girl was conscious. She looked stunned, still flat on her back, arms and legs as before, like an artist's model awkwardly reclined on a divan of crushed moss. Her blue eyes were the color of robin's eggs and showed the minutest sign of movement. They were squinting. At him. Clearly not in admiration. Wyatt, caught off guard, began to compose himself and answer. But before he could muster a reply she rattled off another question:

"And *where* am I?"

Wyatt smiled. "Ah, there, you see, I often ask myself that very same question."

The girl sat up slowly. She stretched her arms and touched her bare knees and white-stockinged legs. She then pinched the frilly red fabric she was wearing.

"And *why* am I wearing a dress? I *hate* dresses."

Her fingers ran over the spongy green stalks she lay upon.

"What *is* this place? And *how* did I get here?"

Wyatt raised a knobby finger. "Ah, more excellent questions!"

"Oh—my—*god*—I'm talking to a frog!"

"Well... I-I," stammered Wyatt, "I do feel I've been influenced by the French. But I've never cared for that crass expression. That moniker... *frog*. The implication, or comparison when—"

"You look like a frog," she told him bluntly.

Wyatt had no rebuttal. The little girl appeared to be unharmed. Which was rather puzzling, having fallen from the sky. She was busy closing her legs and covering her bare knees with her red dress.

"Appearances," he told her, "*can* be deceiving."

She pointed and fired off a bulleted list of his features:

"Webbed feet. Green and red mottled skin. Knobby fingers. Big protruding eyes—"

"All right! *Enough*. You've made your point." Wyatt removed his beret and fanned his flustered face. The sun had risen higher and was making the meadow hot. He was measuring his intakes of air, trying to stay cool, to remain calm. He smiled thinly. "I ask you, how many frogs do you *know* who wear a beret and velvet jacket?"

"One." She told him. "*You*."

"Little girl. And, I assume that *is* what you *are*." Showing he too could be clever, he said, "Pinkish-brown skin. Stringy hair. Tiny nose. White teeth. Pointy fingers. You *are* a girl are you not?"

"What else could I be?"

"Any number of things," he replied. "You are extremely small. I consider *that* an oddity. "

"Maybe it's not me but *you* who are too big."

Wyatt hadn't considered that angle. "Do you have a name?

The girl stood. They were the same height.

"Kat."

"Ahh..." It made perfect sense. She was delirious. "You *think* you are a cat, is that it?"

He was disarmed by her funny little laugh. Released with such abandon. He was enchanted by the pure delight of her sound.

"It's my nickname," said Kat.

"What is?"

"Kat. K. A. T. It's short for Kathlyn."

Wyatt was confused. "Wait. What? Are you saying you were nicknamed 'Kat' because of your diminutive size?"

"*No*. Are all frogs as silly as you?"

"They are *not*. I mean," Wyatt removed his hat to wipe sweat from his face. This was clearly not going the way he had planned. "Now listen. I am *not* silly."

"Then why are you wearing those clothes?"

Wyatt stopped fanning himself. "Excuse me? Do you expect me to go hopping around naked?"

"Isn't that what frogs do?"

Wyatt donned his beret, "I—do *not*."

"You're funny. Your clothes too."

Wyatt flushed. He felt his high pride plummet to the status of a clown. He defended himself with a feeble, "I'm an artist! Of some *esteem* around here. Wyatt. Wyatt T. Frog."

Kat had seen enough. She rubbed her eyes as if they were magic lamps that could grant her a wish to wake from this dream. "I can't believe I'm talking to a frog. Goodbye." She yawned as she rubbed the closed lids of her eyes. When she reopened them she saw things had not changed and scrunched her face with disappointment.

"Hello, again." Wyatt followed her wayward gaze, "I too find it equally puzzling that *I* am talking to a little girl."

Kat pretended to ignore this huge frog. But his splayed red toes were protruding from his sandals and tapping the ground. She bent down and touched the green plumes, semi-transparent and spongy, upon which they both stood. She was tempted to ask what it was.

"Moss," said Wyatt.

She looked into the oblong pupils, before glancing away from his bulging red eyes. She was surrounded by stalks of tall greenery. She rose to the tips of her toes but could not see over the top.

"I'll wake up eventually, I guess."

"You *did* just wake up," Wyatt stated.

This got her full attention as she stared back at him.

With a cavalier smile, a tip of his head, and a touch to his beret, Wyatt said, "Sweet dreams. Good day." He departed by hopping over the hedge of grass. "You may follow me – if you wish!"

"Follow you? A frog? I don't *think* so." Kat folded her arms and refused to accept this nonsense. But, quick to comprehend she didn't have a clue where she was, how she got there, or why she was standing on a mound of enormous moss inside a forest of grass, Kat burst through the curtain of greenery to chase after him.

"Wait!"

His trail was erratic since Wyatt tended to leap after a couple of steps, which left only traces of trampled grass as an indication of his route. The tall stalks of grass tickled her nose as she pushed though. Each stem had fibrous hairs as ticklish as eyelashes and as sticky as a spider's web. She rubbed her face and shouted, "Come back!"

She broke through the forest thicket and came to an open space. A meadow. The day was warm but Kat shivered and hugged herself, pausing to look into the depth of blue sky. She was on the verge of tears. "Mr. Frog? Wyatt, I mean. I'm sorry. About saying those things. About you being silly. I—*ahahh!*"

She shrieked as something sticky sealed her mouth and grasped her arm. She was pulled into a thicket and pinned to the ground.

"Stay still," hissed Wyatt.

"Oh, it's you!" said Kat.

"Shssh." Wyatt held up a fingertip to his lips.

"What are we doing?" she whispered back.

"*Ssshhh.*"

"Are we playing a game?"

"*Ssshhhhhhhhhh.*"

His finger pointed upwards as a shadow passed over them. Kat had the presence of mind to keep her mouth shut but was curious to know why they were hiding and the cause of this darkness. When a horrid noise erupted, causing Kat to cover her ears, she wasn't sure if she wanted to know what it was. The racket finally faded away. She wasn't comfortable being face to face with an enormous frog. Who had bulging eyes and whose eyelids were squinting. Indicating he was still leery. She noticed two bumps between his eyes, also holes, and realized they comprised the sum total of his nose. He had skin that was iridescent and stippled. Green above his wide mouth, white below. He pursed his thin lips. After a few seconds, his mouth parted to emit a subdued croak.

"*Okay.*"

Wyatt stood and brushed off his clothes as he emerged from the thicket. Kat did the same. Her face beamed with a smile, pleased with herself with the knowledge she had retained from school.

"I know what you are. You're a tree frog."

Wyatt, cautiously peering about, said, "I'm sorry, what?"

"Your classification. Species of amphibian."

Wyatt grimaced. "Listen carefully. Do you wish to escape from here unharmed, or not?"

"Well of course I do," said Kat.

"Then stay close, keep quiet, and move quickly. And hide if I tell you to hide."

"Hide from what?"

"Someone you do *not* what to meet. Trust me." Wyatt directed her attention to a standing easel and canvas in the middle of the field. "There, you see. It was not a lie. As I told you, I *am* an artist. A painter of nature's wonders."

"There's nothing there," said Kat.

Wyatt was confused. "You can't see my easel?"

"The canvas is completely blank."

Wyatt nodded thoughtfully. "It might be my greatest work."

Realizing he was joking, she giggled, "You *are* silly."

"It's the fate of all true artists. I advise we depart now."

"What about your easel and paints?"

"I'm afraid they will not be traveling with us."

"Why not?"

"Inanimate objects cannot move about as we do."

"Ha-ha, very funny."

Wyatt cautioned her, "If you plan to come along, stay close to me and do not wander off."

"I'm not some *animal* or—"

"A silly girl?"

Kat gave him a peevish look. She slapped away stalks of grass as they walked. She said to the back of his paint-stained velvet coat, "I hope you're not one of those colorful frogs who secretes poison and can kill by touching."

Wyatt playfully poked her bare arm. "Oh, how I wish."

Kat pulled away.

Wyatt croaked a laugh. "My dear, fear has no relevance here."

"What's that supposed to—hey, wait!"

Kat had to run in spurts to keep up with his long-legged stride. Weaving this way and that, she passed through a maze of tall grass, brushing past curtains of greenery to catch up to him. She found him waiting in a domed clearing, inside a jungle of vibrant growth and bright colors.

"Is this how I get back?" said Kat.

"Back to where?"

"Back home."

"Have you considered this *is* your home? It's home to me."

"Because you're a *frog*."

The lids of his eyes narrowed. "No. Because I am here. As are you. And both of us are here *now*."

"But... Where are we?" She became intrigued by the landscape. Above her were gigantic swells of bright color, like the billowing sails from a fleet of ships puffed out by the wind. Flower blossoms, she realized. Buoyantly they swayed above like helium-filled balloons in a holiday parade. Tulips, carnations, roses. The enormous growth reminded Kat of a story her father had read to her about a boy who climbed a beanstalk to discover a gigantic castle in the clouds. But where was she? If in a dream, it felt too real. And how long before her parents realized she was missing?

As they walked past the craggy face of a cliff Kat realized it was not the side of a mountain but the bark of an enormous pine tree.

"A true artist," said Wyatt, "is devoted to nature."

"Why?" Kat craned her neck to view a cluster of blue tulips.

"Because it is the totality from which all inspiration comes."

Sunlight disappeared as they walked under a gigantic mushroom casting a dank shadow.

"Wonderful," said Kat, treading carefully over the soggy ground. "Like this creepy and gooey humongous umbrella?"

"Mushrooms provide welcome shelter during storms.

Kat pinched her nose. "Augh, it stinks in here."

"Focus on the positive." Wyatt pointed. "See those massive gills? That is where its spores reside and reproduction occurs."

Kat stuck out her tongue. "*Gross.*"

Wyatt chuckled. "This fringed crumble cap mushroom probably thinks you are equally as *gross.*"

"Mushrooms can't think," said Kat.

"*Oh-yes-we-can,*" came a grumble like distant thunder.

"Did you hear that?"

"Mushrooms have feelings too," added Wyatt.

Kat flinched as the mushroom appeared to tilt its massive head. She was glad to escape from its dark shadow into a sparkling tunnel. Through tall ferns the size of palm trees light was streaming down like golden sprinkles of rain.

Wyatt exclaimed, "You see, isn't nature wonderful?"

"Fantastic," Kat said rather glumly.

"Show more enthusiasm. You don't seem very happy."

"Maybe because I'm stuck here with you?"

"Be delighted you exist."

"Wow—okay. I'm overjoyed." Kat produced a saccharin smile

for his benefit. "Is that better?"

"The essence of manufactured sweetness."

Her smile turned sour. "So where are we going?"

"To Evolsdog."

"To *where?*"

Wyatt directed her attention to branches of overhanging foliage. "See those leaves? Power stations. Each one is a sunlight machine. All creations, same as us, thrive from basic elements – light, water, air, minerals. Each one of us is equipped with inventive ways to get what we need."

"You act like this is a field trip," said Kat.

Wyatt pointed to the sky. "Behold, incoming examples of this *gross* byproduct of life."

Through a hole in the interlacing foliage Kat saw what looked to be space capsules floating to earth.

"Dandelion seeds," said Wyatt. "They have parachutes. Each seed was once part of a puffy dome, its structure blown to bits by the wind, now adrift on its own. Each is equipped with little wings for them to glide. Nature is amazingly inventive. Ah, and there's a plant who comes equipped with pods that snap open and shoot their seeds like bullets from a gun."

"You're making this up," said Kat.

"No, that would be the creator. These contraptions are designed for efficient self-propagation. For example, birds find these seeds. The exchange benefits bird and plant. The seeds get swallowed, they take a long ride, and get deposited to the earth elsewhere."

"As poop," said Kat. "Again… *gross.*"

"Gross is a fact of life." Wyatt brushed at spots of paint dried on his jacket. "Not only is nature clever, it also has a sense of humor. I know this one flower who captures and imprisons beetles."

Kat scrunched her lips in disbelief.

Wyatt mimed by grasping vertical bars. "These trapped bugs are held captive inside sticky petals. The flower won't release them until a toll is paid, by giving up a portion of the pollen they have, captured off other flowers. But once the beetles comply, accepting the terms, they get set free, unharmed. A lesson to be learned."

"Flowers and bugs don't think."

"Nor can frogs. Or so you *thought*."

"Maybe it's *me*, my imagination, that's letting let you pretend to think that you are thinking." Kat arched her eyebrows.

Wyatt countered by narrowing his eyelids. "Little girl, you think too highly of yourself. Nature plays no favorites. You are as special to nature – and to me – as an *earwig*."

"Now you're being rude," said Kat.

"As were you, to me." Wyatt removed his beret with a flourish, twirled it theatrically. He repositioned it upon his head with a tilt. "Nature exhibits all the many possibilities that exist for us."

"Yeah," said Kat, "like getting eaten."

Wyatt shrugged. "Well, true. The world is a massive swap meet. A bazaar. A grand redistribution. *Grossly* unpopular at times."

"It's very upsetting to be this small."

"Welcome to my world." Wyatt stopped to rub his chin and to study her. "I wouldn't worry. A predator will likely be confounded and reluctant to swallow you wearing that red dress."

"Or make me a target."

As they continued along the path Kat detected a faint whirring. Something was approaching fast, becoming louder, like a helicopter churning the air. She was suddenly face to face with an iridescent body hovering in the air with a multitude of eyes. Petrified, gulping the same air, she couldn't move. Which starkly contrasted the blur of wings and deafening movement this creature was making.

"What do I do?"

"Stay calm," said Wyatt. "Say hello. You're a curiosity."

"Hel-lo?"

Kat shrieked as she became engulfed by an airstream of motion, circling her 360 degrees, whizzing uncomfortably close, as if sniffing her, before whatever-it-was flew off down the path.

"What—or who—was that?"

"Darlene," said Wyatt with a head shake. "She is a—"

"Dragonfly?"

"She's been called worse."

Wyatt continued to walk. Kat followed beside him.

"I used to be large, you know. Bigger than you. Normal size."

"Normal?" Wyatt waved the concept away. "What's the fun in being normal? Be happy you are *abnormal*."

Kat huffed. "I feel so much better now. Gee, thanks."

"What is big one day will be small the next. There is no rhyme nor reason. Comparisons only confuse. I propose we play a game."

Kat was suspicious. "What sort of game?"

Wyatt bent down, picked up a pine needle and tested its strength. He flipped it in the air, caught it by the thicker end, to be used as a walking stick. "A game that avoids comparisons. Shall we see how far we can get?"

"Not far," said Kat testily. "That would be a comparison."

Wyatt stroked the air with a finger. "You earned a point. You're on your way. Now forget you are small or large, up or down. Good or bad. Ahead or behind."

"How is anyone supposed to win?"

"They cannot. Which is why this game is *so* challenging."

His dry humor caught her by surprise.

Wyatt was charmed by her funny little laugh. "Shall we?"

Kat kicked a pine needle off the path. "Okay, I'll play. As long as you tell me how long it's going to take for us to get to *wherever* it is you said we're going."

Delighted by her irritation, Wyatt said, "A wonderful question. Neither a good nor bad one." He circumnavigated the misty blue sky with a swirl of his pine-needle stick. "Never try to predict the length of time it will take to get anywhere. For you see, it is impossible to calculate the detours and unexpected delays which inevitably occur when traveling from point A to point B. If we try to measure time, we end up wasting it. Treasures of immeasurable pleasure abound, hiding on our path of travel, yet demanding a significant degree of our attention in order to be found."

"Please," said Kat, "just tell me where we're going."

"That *is* the universal question."

"*And?*"

"What?"

"*Where?*"

"First we look for those treasure-troves."

"Treasure troves?"

"Nature speaks to me of these treasures."

Kat was baited to ask, "Nature *speaks* to you?"

"When I listen." Wyatt raised a finger to silence her. "'Watch me as I dance,' whispered the gorgeous maple leaf, 'fallen from the sky to disperse, back to earth, for another chance.' I once lost an entire day staring at a funnel cloud as it twisted and turned into the stem of a tulip, twirling madly about, connecting sky and earth to create a dark purple blossom." Wyatt spun around on his toes looking up. "I was terrified, yet I listened. Do you know what it told me?"

"I can't imagine."

"Guess."

Kat shrugged. "Hello... I'm a tornado?"

"More specific. It told me, 'I am the motion of all things.'"

"You expect me to believe this?"

"Absolutely. We all get screwed up, at times. Whirling about on a destructive path. Exhibiting twisted behavior."

"I don't believe a tornado *talked* to you."

"You're right, it was more a tirade."

"A tirade is a violent long-winded speech. Same thing."

"Well, he *was* very passionate."

"He?"

"Ah, you caught me! Making comparisons." Wyatt winked. "I cannot be certain of its gender. Another point for you."

"This is ridiculous."

"Little Kat, I was attempting to describe something untimely and in the realm of the abnormal. I was *extemporizing*."

"Composing nonsense without preparation. That's the meaning of extemporizing," said Kat.

"Hum, you're smarter than I gave you credit."

"I'm too smart for my own good."

Wyatt frowned. "I highly doubt that."

"My parents think so. They say I'm precocious."

"Precocious?"

"Advanced beyond my age." Kat kicked another pine needle out of her way on the path.

"I know what *precocious* means," said Wyatt.

"I guess that makes us even," Kat teased. "Are frogs smarter than other animals? All loquacious, like you? Meaning—"

"Overly *talkative*," said Wyatt. "That would be a comparison." He stroked the air to give himself a point. "Why did you presume to think that frogs are incapable of thought? And why do your parents think you are precocious? What else do they think you are?"

"Reckless. *Fearless*. Which I'm not. Not really."

"Then why would they say such a foolish thing?"

"My parents aren't foolish!" snapped Kat.

"I've touched a nerve. Since your parents have propagated a girl who, as they claim, is too smart for her own good, I suspect not."

"I don't always *do* what they tell me to do. That's why."

Wyatt was intrigued. "You do the opposite?"

"Not always. And I'm not as bad as other kids I know."

Wyatt stroked the air again. "Tsk, tsk. You made a comparison. My point. Please, an example?"

"Of what?" Kat stopped to dig her heels into the mossy ground. She noticed the fronds were getting shorter and no longer tall enough to tickle her bare arms or legs and knees.

"An example of this *incomparable* behavior of yours."

"I don't know. Like refusing to wear dresses."

"And yet here you are *wearing* a dress."

"Shut up. Talking in classes. Cutting school. Climbing trees. Talking to *frogs?* Is that enough examples for you?"

Wyatt muttered. "Hum. Trees? Interesting."

"Why is that so interesting?"

"The mystery of your existence. It is becoming less of one."

"What are you talking about?"

"Your *path*."

Wyatt surprised Kat by tapping her head with the pine needle stick as if to scold a rather dull student.

"Ouch! That hurt."

"Did it?" He tapped her head again. "How about now?"

Kat held up her hands. "Hey, stop it!"

"I'm making sure you are not dreaming."

"I could be. *Don't*—I said." Kat guarded her head. "What path are you talking about? The one we're on now?"

Kat cowered but Wyatt whacked his own head instead. "No–no–no. Impossible. This path is shrinking – and soon to disappear, to be gone. Become nothing. As you will soon discover."

Kat sighed, shook her head, and covered her face with her hands. "Please let me wake up from this. I want to go home."

"Home is not a destination. It's a state of mind. A journey."

"Whatever." Kat peered through her splayed fingers and saw she was still talking to a frog wearing clothes. She told herself she was dreaming but saw that the mossy path was indeed, as the frog said, progressively narrowing. Or so it appeared. Banks of rock and dirt were on both sides of them now, sloping to a height slightly above her head. Together these two banks formed an odd perspective, lines that tapered and vanished into a distant swirling mist. She heard rushing water that was coming from beyond both banks. She also noticed the flowers and plants along the path were smaller. Almost normal in size. This observation caused Kat to turn and see if the frog had shrunk too.

He had not. His enormous eyes blinked at her.

"What's that?" she asked.

"What is what?"

"The water I'm hearing."

"Yes, it does sound like water. Because it *is*. Rivers, two to be precise, traveling on opposite sides and about to merge. Flowing *exponentially* faster. I assume you know what that word—"

"Progressively faster and faster."

"Soon to merge and become one raging river."

"Then if..." said Kat, "where will we go when they meet?"

"Let us cross that bridge when we get there."

Kat clutched the sides of her dress in frustration.

Wyatt held up four knobby fingers, which required the use of both limbs, since he had but three fingers per hand. "I live by four simple words. Can you guess what they are?"

"Oh—*joy*. A new game."

"Love. Being. Here. Now."

"*Auuggh!* Stop it. You're giving me a headache."

"These words are the key ingredients to finding happiness."

"You are one weird frog."

Wyatt drummed his chin with his knobby fingers as he walked on. "Ah, then you know other frogs, do you? So if..."

Kat could barely hear him over the loud surge of water gushing on both sides and generating an atmosphere of mist.

Wyatt raised his voice, "To answer one of your questions, we are nearing the entrance to Evolsdog."

"Evolsdog? It that where you live?"

Kat wondered if she should be scared. The path led straight into a dense swirling fog. The wall of moisture rose and dispersed into a creamy blue sky. The cool mist intermingled with the sun's warmth and made her skin tingle. She smelled a sugary fragrance. Suddenly she felt weightless, as if walking on an ascending cloud.

The euphoria vanished when the mossy path abruptly ended and became a desolate pointed ridge. A precipice from which a wooden bridge spanned outward. The arc of its suspension vanished midway into an opaque blurry curtain of upwardly-mobile mist. Kat gasped. She grabbed for Wyatt whose knobby fingers took hold of her arm to steady her. On opposite sides rivers were falling, dropping off and merging to crash and form a terrifying waterfall. She was looking down into water surging and curving in a non-stop fall.

Wyatt guided Kat onto the bridge which felt solid, reassuringly firm with thick planks of wood, yet she clung tightly to the railing made from the trunk of a fallen tree. Kat peered over its edge and was captivated by the force of water *falling and curving and falling and curving and falling* – like some ferocious beast hypnotizing her to plunge down with it. This constant colliding water was causing the rising mist. Its opaqueness thinned at intervals, allowing Kat a glimpse of waterwheels churning far below. A multitude of spinning wheels like the ones she imagined turning inside her brain. Her head felt dizzy yet she held on long enough to see that the two rivers, after merging and falling, separated once again far below, traveling apart – around what appeared to be an island.

Wyatt was shouting something at her.

As they got further away from the water's edge, she heard:

"...protective moat! The rivers meet on the other side."

"You live on an island?"

Kat became more curious than nervous as she ventured along the bridge. Verdant foliage now peeked through the mist on the far end. She saw the yellow heads of poplar trees. And hillsides rising into a mountainous spiral like the swirl of vanilla and chocolate ice cream upon a cone, adorned with autumn sprinkles of carmel and mint, all rising into a blue sky with puffy clouds. At its peak she glimpsed, not a cherry, but a glint of something gold.

A shadow swept over them, darkening their world.

Wyatt shouted to her, *"Run!"*

22

Riley Crow

Riley Crow was navigating through the morning sky on a routine mission over Evolsdog. Scrutinizing the rivers and surrounding land mass, he was constantly on a search for signs of insurrection and ready to take action. He was flanked by a squadron of crows, three on each side, all following his lead. Without warning, a bright red object shot through the sky to strike the earth. Riley thought it was a meteorite at first. But no trail of smoke was detected. He dove down to investigate the meadow with his squadron in tight formation, swooping over land which appeared unscorched. Animals scurried into hiding, alarmed by his presence. Riley's objective on these missions was to stir things up and let the lowlanders know they were under surveillance. He took pride in his airborne unit, a disciplined mob, uniformed in black shiny wings as tough as leather but as elegant as flowing capes. Their tapered beaks and booted claws were polished, weapon sharp. They wore helmets to keep themselves hooded and protected against the harsh elements. And to guard against flying debris, their deep-set eyes were goggled. They generated fear like a squadron of spitfires or a motorcycle gang with their raucous squawking as they circled about. Seeing nothing below to entertain them, they flew off, disgruntled.

Riley took rest by landing in the tallest pine tree on the topmost branch. His crew fought and jostled for position on the lower limbs. Their commotion agitated his mind and he let out a nasty squawk. He was trying to ignore the turbulent visions that haunted him 24/7. He found it impossible to sit still long. As hard as he tried, he could not shake the strange notion that he was something other than what he was – a crow. He pecked at his feathers, as if to fix and disguise visible flaws, obsessively inspecting for chinks in his armor. Any sign of weakness could destroy his leadership. He had a phobia of losing power, which he sensed was mentally eroding him like some poison, eating away at his churning gut too. He flinched at the phantom flickers of gunfire and screams coming from nameless faces smeared like blood across the dark interior of his mind – causing him to lurch off the branch.

Taking flight helped dispel these spectors that pestered his mind and blindsided him each time he stopped to rest. He had a nagging suspicion that something wasn't right in the world, which made him soar off toward the island. His squad, caught off guard dozing and preening, were now struggling with frantic wing-beats to catch up and reassemble behind him.

Riley's instincts had proven correct. A breach in security was in progress. He spotted Wyatt T. Frog aiding and abetting the enemy – attempting to smuggle a foreign entity dressed in red through the gates of Evolsdog.

Kat was running to keep up with Wyatt who was nearly midway across the bridge when Riley swooped down in front of them. He made his grand entrance theatrically costumed in his flowing cape, as if alighting onto a stage, landing with aplomb to intervene. His cronies clattered behind him onto the bridge's railing and walkway. With a critical glance at his supporting cast, his chorus of buffoons, Riley tucked his wings behind his back and looked darkly upon the intruders through the mask of his hooded eyes.

"Well—well—*well*..." Riley squawked.

Wyatt was annoyed by the intrusion. "Get out of my way."

"And *what* have we here?

"A girl. I found her in the meadow."

"You *found* her? Like a stray pet you decided to keep?"

"She's lost," said Wyatt. "I am trying to help her."

"Oh I see *that*." Riley's said pointedly, "You *know* the rules."

"Your rules, you mean," said Wyatt.

"Precisely." With no further explanation needed, Riley poked his beak at Kat for a closer inspection – startling her.

"Leave her alone," said Wyatt.

"And why would I do that?" Riley circled Kat. "This *creature* does not belong here."

"Back off," said Wyatt.

"Look how *tiny* she is." Riley, taller than both Wyatt and Kat, lowered his head and poked his nose into her face. "The operative word here is small. Or little. *Petite.*"

Wyatt stepped between them, "Point taken, Riley. Her size and appearance here is unusual, I agree. But—"

"Caw-ha!" Riley crowed, "You agree! She is *not* one of us."

Wyatt appeared nonchalant but his fingers balled into fists inside his pockets. "Stop trying to win all the time."

"Homeland security *is* about winning — *all* the time." Riley's beady eyes darkened, challenging Wyatt with a militant squint.

In his pockets Wyatt found acorns he had brought for lunch. The nubs of his fingers scooped them up to serve as a peace offering. Riley eyed the nuts suspiciously. Wyatt tossed them onto the bridge and Riley jumped back in alarm as if they were miniature grenades. The acorns scattered and rolled about and the other crows squawked and shielded themselves with their wings.

When nothing exploded, the crows dove to confiscate the nuts. Except for Riley, who squawked:

"Stop, lads! Those nuts may be poisoned!"

"Oh-my-*God*." Kat was unable to contain her amusement and blurted a little laugh, quickly covering her mouth.

Riley thrust his face at her as if threatening to bite her head, snapping, then opening his beak. "What is so funny?"

She was tickled by the realization. "You. You're a crow!"

Riley took umbrage. "I... am the Gatekeeper!"

"And resident *pest*," added Wyatt.

"*Protector* of Evolsdog," clarified Riley.

"Town *bully*," grumbled Wyatt.

"Head of *security*."

"Thug!"

"Chief of Police!"

Wyatt sighed, "Why is she a threat?"

"Look what she's wearing." Riley scowled. "It's a *red* flag!"

Kat pinched the sides of her dress. "It's a pinafore."

"Pin–a–fore!? She's speaking in code!"

"A pinafore—you fool," said Wyatt, "*is* a dress."

Riley hopped over to squawk at his comrades. "Why was I not informed of this? Why—Why—Why?"

Wyatt took advantage of their squabbling by grasping Kat by the arm to sneak past them. Riley spun around.

"Halt! You are *not* to walk. Only *talk*. "

"Get out of my way," said Wyatt.

"You call that a threat?" Riley mocked. "About as threatening as your art. What is it? Surrealism? Abstraction? Impressionistic? Like you, Wyatt. You exist in concept only. Caw-ha!"

Wyatt managed a smile. "Let's see what Wick has to say."

"Wick!?" Riley began to hop from side to side to prevent Wyatt and Kat from advancing. "Wick is an ignoramus."

"Who's Wick?" asked Kat.

"No concern of *yours*," said Riley. "Who are *you*?"

"I'm Kat," said Kat.

"Liar," said Riley. "You are not a *cat*."

"Wick is our Prime Minister," said Wyatt.

"And an *imbecile*." Riley stopped to rest.

"That's a rude thing to say of someone," said Kat."

"Is it? Then let me rephrase," said Riley, "our Prime Minister is mentally *deficient*."

"That's saying the same thing," Kat said.

Riley cackled, "Right you are! Our Prime Minister is a *complete* moron! I am beginning to warm to this little girl, Wyatt."

"May we proceed?" said Wyatt.

"*Wait–wait–wait.*" Riley expanded his wings to duck his head and scratch his nose against the collar of his cape to signal he was contemplating the matter. "There have been rumors. *Stories* of these sorts of occurrences. A little girl *now*. But once inside—oh yes!—she could blow up—become huge—gigantic! *She* could be a virus created to destroy us all!"

"Or…" said Wyatt, "this could be your paranoia talking."

Riley snapped back, "My—*what!?*"

"Irrational fear and distrust of others," said Kat.

Riley snarled at her, "I *know* that! Do you know what the word *rhetorical* means? My reaction was to insinuate that *if* your colorful new *pal* here ever calls me that again… he… well, he had better *not*. You lack the foresight to comprehend the things I have seen."

"What are you implying?" said Wyatt.

"Seeing you, sneaking into the outer woods and meadows where it's forbidden to go! Where you can be seen by you-know-*who*."

"Who?" said Kat.

Riley ignored her. "You have become a *liability*."

"Meaning?" said Wyatt.

"You're a subversive. What's your real game, Wyatt?"

Wyatt indicated Kat. "As I told you, I'm simply trying to—"

Riley spun around, acting like an interrogator at an inquisition. "Admit it, Wyatt! You are an undercover agent engaged in a covert operation to expose and destroy Evolsdog!"

"Don't be an idiot," said Wyatt.

"Confess it!"

"Or what? Have me tortured?"

Riley reeled on his booted heels to laugh. "There is no *need* for that kind of accusation. Torture is a sad misconception. Like death. And each poor soul who is brought back to the illusion of having *had* a life? Few are very pleased about their revival, I can assure you. I receive top security reports from informants. Reliable sources to confirm my findings. To justify torture!"

"Are you finished?" said Wyatt.

"Once you have admitted to being a spy," said Riley.

"I'm an *artist*," said Wyatt.

"I've tortured others for less," said Riley.

The crows burst into raucous laughter and hopped about.

"Tear them to shreds, lads! Caw-ha!"

As the crows crept forward Wyatt removed his beret and flung it off the bridge. The crows compulsively dove after it. Wyatt shook his head and told Kat, "Riley can be incredibly irritating."

"Are we in danger?" she asked.

"Riley is a danger only to himself."

The crows reemerged on the bridge squabbling as Riley chastised them for abandoning their posts. "You're on report! Tricked by an evasive tactic. A classic textbook technique used by all self-admitted artists. Whose vocation, by definition, is to manipulate, to deceive!"

This unruly behavior reminded Kat of an incident at home, when a murder of crows had flown down to toy with her pet labrador who was sleeping in their backyard. The crows kept flying down to peck at its head. As if in play. Bullying, really The memory incited Kat to step forward and poke Riley's feathered coat from behind.

"Why are you so nasty?"

Riley squawked and swung around. "Who says I am?"

"I do. You're a crow, aren't you?"

Riley sensed her question to be a ruse. "What if I was?"

"Crows are supposed to be smart," said Kat.

Riley beamed. "Then I *must* be a crow."

"Then why are you acting just the opposite."

Wyatt croaked a laugh.

Riley bristled, pausing to smooth his ruffled feathers, pretending to be unfazed. "Have you heard the adage about those who reach the pinnacle of intelligence? It goes like this: The sharper one becomes, the quicker they can *snap!*"

Kat jumped back as Riley snapped his beak at her.

"So back off, little girl!"

Kat blanched, fearing for her life.

"Caw-ha!" Riley squawked, "Cat got your tongue?"

"Leave her alone," said Wyatt.

Riley flung his goggles back to glare at Kat. "Scared?"

"A little, yes," she admitted.

"Good. Consider *fear* your friend."

"What is that supposed to mean?" challenged Kat.

Riley brought his head close to hers. "Fear keeps you safe."

Kat held her ground.

Riley raised his head, arching an eyebrow. "A friend you *hate*, and wish to lose – but need to have around."

"I suppose like you?" said Kat. "Thanks, but no thanks."

Riley was bemused. "Wee girl, do you *bite* too?"

Clattering onto the railing flew a crow with Wyatt's beret held in its beak. Riley snatched it. "What are you – a dog? You fetch like one." Riley tossed Wyatt his hat. He swung back at Kat. "And *you*. What are you? A cat? Hah! Pretending to be this—this—*little* girl. What's up with that?"

"But I *am* a—"

"Silence! Look at where you stand."

Riley pointed with an outstretched wing toward the meadow. "Upon the cusp of time. The ghost of yesterday not far behind." He swung his other wing toward the swirling mist at the opposite end of the bridge. "With your tomorrow cascading ahead, yet misaligned."

"Stop being dramatic," said Wyatt.

"I wasn't talking to *you*."

"Misaligned?" said Kat.

"You are positioned wrongly in time," said Riley.

Kat looked forward then backward. "Are you saying this bridge and waterfall represents present time, where I am now, as opposed to my past and future?"

"Precisely," nodded Riley. "It was a metaphor."

"Make your point," said Wyatt.

"I am *making* my point," said Riley.

"Are you telling me to choose which way to go?" said Kat.

"No–no–no," Riley hopped for emphasis. "You have reached the point of no return. You are not meant to be here *nor* there!"

"Then *where* I am supposed to be?"

"You are *missing* the point."

Kat cupped a hand to whisper to Wyatt, "Is he mad?"

"Yes–I–am–mad!" cried Riley. "You keep missing my *point*."

"But Mr. Crow—"

"Riley."

"Riley," said Kat. "I can't see your point."

"The point *is*…" Riley sighed. "You do *not* want to enter."

"Then *where* am I supposed to go!?"

"Again—*not* the point." Riley threw up his wings.

"I feel more lost than ever," sighed Kat.

"Good," said Riley. "In order to be found you need to be *lost*. Finally, you are getting somewhere."

Kat shot back, "I am getting nowhere—thanks to you!"

"Poppycock, you are making tremendous progress."

Kat clutched her head and shook it, "This is all very confusing. When I woke up I didn't know where I was, or how I got here. Now I'm beginning to wonder if I even know *who* I am."

"Caw-ha, stupendous!" crowed Riley. "Now you are—"

"Oh, be quiet!" Kat pushed past Riley, squawking with the other crows who fluttered noisily but parted as she walked to the center of the bridge. She stopped to observe both the swirling mist rising and water falling. The sensation made her feel as if she was riding on a platform ascending into heaven.

Wyatt approached from behind with a hop-skip-and-a-jump.

She asked him, "What did you say this place was called?"

Wyatt pointed towards an arched sign spanning the far end of the bridge. It was partially obscured by the swirling mist. Sunlight shone on the letters that said:

EVOLSDOG

Riley reappeared, materializing through the mist to swoop down and land on the railing beside them.

"Not *you* again," said Kat.

"Me again," said Riley.

"Please don't tell me you're coming along."

Riley narrowed his eyes. "I will *not* be coming along."

"You're lying," said Kat.

"I am telling you what you wanted to hear."

Wyatt whispered to her, "You see what I wanted to avoid?"

Riley began preening his feathers, but stopping to say, "Enter at your own risk. You have been forewarned. It is my sworn duty to protect and serve. The reason I am *here* is for your own good."

Kat scoffed, "As in someone to fear?"

Riley chuckled. "I like her, Wyatt. She is feisty!"

34

Izzy Beaver

Izzy Beaver was seated in a wicker chair on the deck of his grotto lodge which was situated inside a cave, beneath a cliff, and reinforced by an infrastructure of timber. His self-made home had a most unusual view. It faced a sheer wall of cascading water. This constant fall of water created a humid and misty climate, an atmosphere Izzy enjoyed. The roar of white noise complemented the hideaway ambience of his home. His fingers were crooked around a mug of steaming coffee while the sharp nails of his other paw were clasped to a cinnamon biscotti, being gnawed by his protruding incisors.

His sanctuary was abruptly ruptured by a contraption tearing into the sparkling liquid curtain – accompanied by a garbled yelp – which came and went. Both object and sound were obliterated and drowned out by the waterfall.

Izzy spilled his coffee, dropped his biscuit—lurching to his feet.

"Sun of 'clipse," he groused, shuffling across the deck to clutch the railing only a short distance from the downpour of water.

"Tart 'n feathers!" He grasped the railing and tore his claws into the wood. He ground his teeth, griping incoherently while glaring into the wall of liquid. He was exhausted. He had worked through the night installing another hydraulic wheel to the power grid and was in desperate need of some peace – and sleep.

"Dam–'t–all," he grumbled, prior to diving into the thundering force of water to rescue whomever it was who had fallen.

After a downward pummeling Izzy regained his equilibrium and maneuvered his way through the rapids. His vision wasn't the best, but underwater Izzy was adept at swimming around these rock solid obstacles and avoiding collisions. He spotted a whirlpool of light up ahead and surfaced within a relatively calm pocket of shallow water. Which was where he found Angelo Iguana along with the debris of wreckage from some contraption scattered upon an inlet of sand.

Izzy swam up to Angelo whose pale green body was twisted and impelled against a jagged rock. His bright orange jumpsuit was torn, the sleeves shredded. His legs were badly injured and half of his tail was missing. He appeared to be unconscious. Izzy ascertained from the wreckage – spotting fragments of a propeller and segments from what appeared to have once been wings – that it was the result of another failed adventure. To attain flight!

"Rudder sucker," he cursed. He slapped his tail flat upon the sand, angered by his friend's reckless disregard for life and limb. The contraption his friend had built was beyond recovery. His breakfast and morning relaxation was also unrecoverable. But ingrained with a commitment to duty and a strong work ethic, Izzy lifted Angelo's head to apply mouth-to-mouth resuscitation. He cleared the blue tongue from his throat, then placed his whiskered mouth to his friend's scaly blue lips to blow air into the lungs. Izzy zipped open Angelo's flight jacket and pumped his chest. He then went back to forcing air into his mouth. Izzy's efforts after pumping and blowing stimulated a spout of murky water to erupt like a tiny geyser.

Angelo gasped and wheezed. "I'm okay." He raised a limp arm to wave at the nonexistent crowd of onlookers roaring in a cascade of support for his efforts. "Thank you all for coming."

"Idiot," cursed Izzy, "you are *not* okay."

Angelo blinked, slowly gaining focus on Izzy's dripping wet face. "Izzy? Is that you? It worked. I flew!"

Izzy spit into the rocks. "You crashed, ya fool!"

"Only afterwards." Angelo struggled to sit up. "Oooh-*ouch*."

"Look at yourself. You lost your tail. *Again*."

"It grows back." Angelo smiled, wincing as he moved to support his torso against a boulder.

"Doubtful you can stand," said Izzy.

Angelo examined his torn jumpsuit and mangled limbs. His legs were angled not as they were intended to be, but turned radically inward. "Give me a sec." Angelo grasped the bolder and struggled to hoist his body upwards. The effort made his eyelids collapse and his body drop like a sack of beans onto the sand bar.

"Suds 'n a beach!" Izzy wasted no time in lifting his unconscious friend over his shoulder and lugging him across the rocky landscape. The booted soles of his feet were as tough as the uneven terrain and Izzy had Angelo at the gateway of his residence within minutes. The tremendous shower and spray from the waterfall didn't faze Izzy, in fact he loved it, dripping wet again as they advanced over stepping stones that led to his cave hidden behind the barrier of falling water. He laid Angelo down upon floorboards inside the cage of a hydraulic elevator. The mechanism was constructed from renewable parts of wood and twine and metal. Izzy slammed his fist against the switch. Which shot them vertically into the air guided by a system of pulleys. After zooming several seconds they slowed to a precise stop at the base of a bridge. The entrance to Evolsdog.

Izzy kicked open the cage door. With Angelo hoisted over his shoulder he walked onto the cobblestone street and deposited him in a heap at the base of a monolithic tower. A totem pole housing a polished bronze bell at its spire. It rang noisily as Izzy yanked its chain. The clanging racket roused the town and soon all residents were emerging to peer from their storefronts and homes. As well, it jolted Angelo out of his stone-cold state of unconsciousness.

Awakening at this way station, a place Angelo had become all too familiar with of late, he shifted his head to rest upon a groomed patch of moss and waved his arm at the crowd assembling. "Thanks for your support. I'm okay. I'll be fine."

"Says you," said Izzy, spitting in a flower bed. "Look at yourself. You used to be somebody. Now look at ya."

"I am still somebody, Izzy." Angelo smiled, though feeling dazed.

Why his fans who supported his efforts kept moving past him like he was yesterday's garbage made him curious, craning his neck

– which took great effort since his legs were not working properly –
to see the phenomenon himself.

A little girl!

She was standing at the foot of the bridge beside Wyatt T. Frog
and Riley Crow. Even Izzy promptly abandoned Angelo to enquire
about the source of this commotion.

"Mother pumpkin!" Izzy exclaimed.

"Go on without me," Angelo encouraged with a wave.

Izzy pushed his way through the crowd of idle watchers to get
right to the point of the disturbance by walking up to this anomaly.
He pulled at his whiskers and tucked the claws of both paws around
the straps of his overalls and declared, "Well if eggs don't beat all.
Where in torn nation did *you* come from?"

"Excuse me?" said Kat.

"Kat, I'd like you to meet Izzy," said Wyatt.

Izzy gave Kat a no nonsense once-over assessment. "Good *glob*
– if you aren't a wee bit of a thing-a-ma-gig."

His words baffled her. "Are you... a beaver?"

"Would it make a hill of bees if I was or wasn't? No."

"You're not?"

"Of course I am! What are you?"

"A girl." Kat rubbed the fabric of her dress with her thumb and
fingers to calm herself while she looked toward Wyatt for help.

The frog gave her a thin smile and a squint of reassurance. "Izzy
has a unique relationship with words."

"Hats 're a fact," said Izzy. "Never seeds the likes of somebody
with your kinda growth."

"I woke up here," said Kat. "Which was a surprise for me."

"Fingers as much." Izzy rubbed his teeth with a fingernail.

Kat braved a smile and stared at the assemblage of creatures –
rabbits, possums, skunks – who looked as shocked to see her as she
was to see them. All were standing upright, wearing clothing and

strangely the same height as herself. Among the crowd she saw the long face and shadowy eyes of a baboon who was studying her as he puffed smoke from a pipe. Several mice, looking like schoolchildren, one holding a soccer ball, were outfitted in matching jerseys and all tittering. A skittish-looking tarsier with its wide eyes was clutching flowers that shook. The white-feathered cockatoo sporting a yellow mohawk widened her black beak to let out a screech.

What kept Kat calm was the warm surroundings of the village. It was an equally bright and shady place nestled among redwoods at the base of a hill that rose from trees into a spiraling steep mountain. Kat stood on cobblestones that appeared to be the main street which led through an assortment of quaint buildings constructed from river rocks and timber. Each structure appeared unique and yet there was an overall feeling of uniformity. She saw the many arched windows, slated roofs, shingled walls. She noticed an ornate spiral staircase ascending into a tree. The cobblestones cut a path through the town to form a valley. Beyond were streets that branched off and wound uphill past homes adorned with flower boxes. From this valley floor two slopes emerged to spiral into a mountain peak. Spangled leaves from dark green oaks and golden poplars adorned the foothills. Far above, upon the mountain ridge, Kat saw a cluster of color.

She gazed overhead into the sky, a place more familiar than this quaint little village. She recalled lying on her back upon the slanted roof of her home, her mind drifting with the white cumulus clouds overhead and realizing her body too was as mutable as a cloud. When she looked back down from the sky, Kat was struck by an odd sensation. It was as if she was standing inside a storybook.

Izzy whistled. "Somebody sure done cats a *spell* on you, girl."

"Excuse me?" said Kat

"Her name *is* Kat," said Wyatt.

Izzy expelled another whistle. "If rats don't take the cake."

"And," Riley announced, "she is under arrest!"

Kat blinked. "I am?"

Izzy yawned. "I too could use some rest."

"I said arrest!" said Riley.

Izzy rubbed his eyes and blinked.

"Wake up!" said Riley, "I caught Wyatt trying to smuggle this *creature* in here. But I intervened – stopping them!"

Izzy scratched his whiskers. "But you've let the girl inside."

Riley stiffened, tucking back his wings. "That is here nor there, she is now under my surveillance."

"Okay, swell, then I'm off to take that nap," said Izzy.

"No!" said Riley. "There could be an insurrection!"

"An insurrection?" said Izzy.

"She could blow up the entire power grid."

"The power grid!?" Izzy shook off his drowsiness and reassessed Kat with a vigorous squint. "You'd *do* that?"

"Yes!" said Riley.

"No," said Kat. "What's a power grid?"

"See how clever she is?" Riley stomped. "So sly! *Insidious.*"

"I am not *insidious* – or harmful," said Kat.

"Says who? *You?*" squawked Riley.

"It's Riley's paranoia talking," said Wyatt.

"Stop saying that!" Riley ruffled his cape of wings.

"Feather 't down," said Izzy. "Who's this Para Nora?"

"Nobody," said Wyatt. "This girl is simply lost."

"How'd you become this wee bit-a-of-thing?" Izzy asked.

"Honestly," Kat said, "I wish I could tell you."

"Because," said Riley, "she *refuses.*"

"No! Because I don't know," said Kat.

"Hell's bells," said Izzy. "Then where'd ya come from?"

Wyatt interjected. "I saw her fall from the sky."

"She fell from the sky!?" said Izzy.

"Like a comet!" Riley dashed Kat's head with his wing.

"Hey!" Kat straightened her mussed hair.

"Smack dab into Twain River meadow!" Riley gave a nod to Izzy who gave Wyatt a suspicious squint.

"Why'd ya vent yourself so fur beyond the gates?"

Wyatt clenched the top of his pine needle. "I went to paint."

"Paint?" spat Izzy. "Ain't no homes need of *paint'n* out there."

"On a *canvas*. I'm an artist. Remember?"

Riley said, "So show us this supposed *art* you painted."

"I left it all there. My brushes, paints, along with the easel."

"Why'd ya take the *weasel?*" said Izzy.

"An *easel*. It holds the canvas." Wyatt tipped his walking stick toward Kat. "I left everything there to help guide this girl here."

"I saw his canvas. It's true," said Kat with a tentative a smile.

"Who asked you?" said Riley.

Izzy tapped his incisors with the tips of his pointed fingernails. "You don't belong here, young lady. Not like *this*, you don't."

"Like what?" Kat appealed. "I only want to go home."

"So do I." Izzy stretched and yawned. "Been up *all* night."

"Are you the Prime Minister?" asked Kat.

"No, Wick is," said Wyatt. "Izzy's the Chief Engineer."

Izzy tugged at his overalls. "I run the works around here."

Riley lifted his goggles. "But who *protects* the works? Me!"

Izzy huffed. "I'm a fixer. Things break, I fix 'em."

Kat asked him, "Can you fix, I mean, help me get home?"

"Are you broken?"

"I don't think I am."

"I can't fix ya if ya ain't broke."

Izzy pulled out a hammer from his tool belt like it was a pistol. Held by its claw, he brandished and pointed the wooden shaft down the street. "You bust a gut, you go see Doc Owen. You aim to break a leg on stage, you go see Scarlet. You lose your nut, go see Hazel. To unravel your mind, ya go see Zhena. But stay clear of Camille, you hear?"

"Why? Who's—"

"She's a shade of something not quite there. Ya can't fix that."

"She means well," said Wyatt. "We think."

Izzy holstered his hammer. "Little girl, not only did I build the grid, I invented it." He took out a tape measure to scratch the hook against his forehead as if erasing something, then extended its blade to point with it up the hill. "If truth be gold – which it certainly *is* – the source of wisdom came from Prater, the professor. Who lives up yonder, inside a gold box."

Kat glimpsed a golden sparkle at the top of the mountain.

Izzy added, "But it's me, I tell ya, who created iconometric."

Kat asked politely, "What is that?"

"Negative mixing with the positive. Yin-yang. Heard 'f it?"

"Yes, but... that makes no sense."

Izzy groused, "Nor do *you*. How's you get to be so small?"

"I was born this way."

The congestion of onlookers was tightening around them.

Izzy took from his tool belt a slab of stone to spit on. He pulled out a buck knife and held it aloft. The crowd backed away. With a chuckle he began to grind the blade. "You hit the *snail* on its head. Things don't happen with no reason. It's gotta rhyme. Make sense to the dollar. Knows how I mean? Needs to fit. Together."

"I guess. But..." Kat looked at Wyatt for help.

"But you do *not!*" Izzy pointed the knife at Kat.

"That's enough," said Wyatt, stepping between them.

Izzy leveled his knife at Wyatt's throat. "Whose side ya on? Stay away from me ya green-horned *toad*."

"He's a tree frog." Kat quickly regretted saying it.

Izzy swung the blade at her. "I'm a *dam* site exhausted, *Missy*, and liable to burst. So don't open my flood gates! Riley, keep this *frog* from hopping in my face again. And do your due diligence and instigate a measure of crowd control around here! *Pronto!*"

Riley squawked at his squad of crows who descended from the trees to land beside him. Four hustled back the crowd. The other two flew off with Riley after a brief consultation.

Izzy rubbed his eyes with the back of his paw, then refocussed his fuzzy eyesight on Kat. "You think you can just *waltz* into our world where you don't belong? It ain't proper. It ain't!"

"But I didn't—"

"What!?" said Izzy. "Come here to infiltrate?"

"*No*," said Kat.

"Blow up the *power* grid?"

"*No*. I don't *care* about your stupid power grid!"

A collective gasp arose from the crowd which startled her.

Izzy stabbed his knife into a sign post. "What'd ya say?"

"Nothing. I didn't mean anything."

"Every cog has to fit to function," said Izzy. "To have a purpose. No, not *you*. You fell from the sky – like a lose cog – like a – like a – a *wench* thrown in to bust my gears."

Kat cried, "But I don't want to even be here!"

"Poppy-talks!" Izzy dug his claws into her arm.

"Ouch," said Kat, "that hurts. Let go of me!"

Izzy tugged her through the congestion of onlookers who parted as his other arm pointed this way and that. "Gardener. Merchant. Seamstress. Cook. Carpenter. *Crook!*" Izzy aimed his forefinger at a skulking skunk. "You owe me big time, Stinky."

The skunk scuttled off. He lifted his tail in a rude gesture.

"Waste collector," explained Izzy. "But *you*, little girl—"

"My name is Kat," said Kat.

"Cat?" said Izzy. "You ain't no *cat*. If Riley has his eye on you, then so do I. I aim to find out *why* you came, *what* it is you want, and *who* sent you."

"Ouch, you're hurting me!" Kat looked for Wyatt.

More town creatures had come to gather and ogle.

Izzy growled, "She's under my jurisdiction! So back off!"

Riley flew down to land beside Izzy. He scampered and hopped to keep up with the beaver's fast pace. "She's mine, Izzy! You have no right to keep her!   Finders keepers."

Izzy swiped his metal ruler at Riley. "Be useful. Go get Wick!"

"*Wick?* Wick's useless. He has no opinions. He—"

"That's why we *need* him," said Izzy. "Now go!"

Riley griped but pulled down his goggles and flew off.

Izzy clutched down on Kat's arm. She cried out as he trudged her down the street. Wyatt was pushing to get past the throng who were trailing behind Izzy and Kat like debris from a comet. The mob was so thick and tightly bound Wyatt had no room to bend his legs and leap above them.

Angelo Iguana was on a collapsible gurney as the horde passed, being lifted onto a flatbed cart by two raccoons in white uniforms. One of the paramedics stayed in back to secure Angelo while the other hopped behind the wheel into a buggy seat. The driver wrung his paws compulsively, cleaning them, before he powered up the steam engine, sending puffs of billowing white smoke into the air.

"What about him?" asked Kat, pointing to the iguana.

"What about who?" huffed Izzy.

"If everyone here is a cog that fits," said Kat, "then—"

"Village *idiot*," snorted Izzy. "Every town needs one."

Wyatt landed on his feet a few paces in front of Izzy, pleased with his acrobatic feat, but was pushed aside by Izzy moving fast.

"That *lizard* calls himself an inventor. *Haugh*—I say!"

"What does he invent?" Kat was trying to make conversation while being yanked along, hoping this beaver would take pity on her.

"Nothing. Not a *dam* thing that's ever worked worth a dam."

"Then why—"

"Angelo's a risk taker. Takes risks. Risky. I admire that."

"Ouch," said Kat.

"Am I hurting you?"

"Yes."

"Good. Life is supposed to hurt. According to Angelo."

"Who?"

"Ya got *bats* in your ears? That crazy lizard. Used to be right in the mind," chided Izzy. "He's ill equipped, yet determined to fly. Angelo's that *thing* who thinks he has feathers."

"Oh," said Kat. "I know. From that poem?"

"Poem? Who we talking about?"

"My mother used to recite it. The thing with feathers? It means someone who has hope."

"No it don't," muttered Izzy. "It means he's a *dam* fool."

The vehicle transporting Angelo chugged past them and the injured iguana seemed at peace, as if traveling to his coronation, or funeral, and gave Kat a dignified yet restrained wave since his wrists were synched down by straps.

Kat waved back with her free hand.

As the ambulance ventured up the hill, from behind it appeared a most unusual apparition. It appeared to be dressed entirely in blue. Body and face too, in similar hues. Izzy stopped in his tracks and blurted out a garbled expletive and changed his trajectory.

"Oh, you–who, *Izzy!* I've been looking all over for you!"

Both Izzy and Kat stopped. The crowd behind them too. Which allowed Wyatt to hop up beside them.

"Are you okay?" he asked.

Kat said, "Does it look like I am? Who or what – is that?"

"Hello, Camille," said Wyatt, touching his beret.

"Where are we all traveling to in such a *mad* rush?"

Kat realized this blue thing was a woman. The sheer gown she wore flowed and floated like an ethereal cloud nestled around her body. She had a svelte physique with delicate, if not anorexic, limbs.

Her movement seemed unsteady, her arms wavering as if to help her navigate through a sultry breeze. Yet there was no wind. Her face was obscured by a veil of fabric attached to her hat that resembled a tiny wedding cake. Her head was disproportionately larger than her slender body. Except for her long tail coiled tightly like the swirl of a fern shoot. Yet her eyes, Kat realized, were the most disconcerting, moving and protruding independently like gyroscopes.

Izzy stammered, "C-c-can't you *see* I'm busy, Camille?"

"Izzy, you are *always* on the move. Slow down and accompany me on my next grand excursion."

"A tempting offer. I'll be sure to con fritter it."

"And *who*—pray tell—is *this?*"

"This is Kat," said Wyatt.

"A cat?" said Camille. "How very curious. I suppose you could be. I do see a resemblance."

"Are you…" said Kat. "Aren't you a chameleon?"

"*Camille.*" Her gloved hand, shaped like a claw, touched Kat's chin. "I am many things, darling."

"That we know," said Izzy. "Nice to see ya, gotta go."

"Always in a rush." Camille rolled her eyes and unfurled her tail, turning her head to address Kat. "To be elsewhere. Except with me. I travel, you see. Yesterday I was in Venice."

"Italy?" Kat was pleased to hear someplace she recognized.

Wyatt quietly shook his head at Kat.

"The length of my stay, who can say. But it was *magnifique!*"

"She's never been anywhere," whispered Wyatt.

"Greece, Spain, Moscow, next a safari. In Africa—imagine that! My itinerary is over-booked. Overly full."

"That sounds… exciting," said Kat to be polite.

"But I want to hear about you. Where did *you* come from?

She glanced at Wyatt. "I fell from the sky."

"Are you from the moon? I have been meaning to go there."

"No surprise," grumbled Izzy. "Now, excuse us—"

"Gravity here can be *so* overwhelming. Don't you agree?"

Izzy pulled Kat by the arm. "Like I told ya, gotta go."

Camille snapped, "Don't you walk away from me!"

Izzy shouted back, "I can—will—and *am*."

Glancing over her shoulder Kat saw Camille change color from a placid aqua to a vibrant green. Her hands were balled into fists. And her eyes whirling before realigning on Kat. "And—*why*—her? Why—is—she—here!?"

"It's best we keep moving," said Izzy.

Kat was struck on her neck by something sticky – which pulled her backwards.

Izzy dug his claws into her arm. "Hold on!"

Kat panicked when she saw a wad of purple attached to her.

"Camille! *Dam* you! Let her go!"

Izzy lost his grip on Kat. She screamed, dragged backwards over the cobblestones until stopped by Wyatt who leapt in front of her to prevent further movement. Suctioned to Kat's neck was Camille's tongue and he yanked it off. The wad of flesh sprung like a rubber band pulled taut and released – whipping through the crowd. Until sucked back into the chameleon's mouth.

Shocked by the ordeal, Kat felt her neck. She examined the claw marks to her arm. Blood was oozing from her skin.

"You're hurt," said Wyatt.

"It's not that bad," said Kat.

She was much more concerned and curious about this creature, Camille, who was now sauntering away. Her entire body had turned a mustard yellow.

Wyatt helped Kat to her feet.

Izzy came back to repossess her arm.

Kat asked them, "Why did she attack me?"

The beaver pulled her along. "Cause ya don't belong here."

50

Hazel Squirrel

52

Hazel Squirrel would have come outside to partake in the excitement had she heard the bell clang in the tower. But she had been underground rooting inside the cellar of her tree shop searching for a specific nut she would eventually locate. But by the time she resurfaced to the showroom, it was empty. Not of trinkets, all were there, polished and shiny, nothing out of place, aligned on shelves and tables as they had been. Only of customers. They had disappeared. Vanished. As if they had been misplaced.

Moments before, her fashionable shop had been bustling with avid shoppers. This sudden departure was quite unsettling to Hazel. So she did the only thing she knew what to do at times of unease to calm herself. She reached for her feather duster and began to dust. This disappearance and abandonment was one more reminder that uncertainty presaged certain disaster.

From her boutique inside the hollow of an ancient redwood tree, she skittered about, dusting this and that, works of art, each item, until making her way over to the entrance. Where she peeked out the door. To an empty street. Another oddity to unsettle her nerves. She extended an arm to dust the engraved letters upon an ornately carved sign. It hung from a pole and extended like the branch of a tree with a four-letter word that defined her boutique:

NUTS.

The interior space was her own design. It had hardwood floors. Its tall circular walls were richly rustic yet lined with row upon row of smooth polished shelving carved from maple. The room sparkled with miniature glass fixtures suspended on fibers at various lengths emerging from the dark ceiling to resemble an evolved community of spiders who, having dropped down, were each equipped with a light. A vertical ladder was attached to tracks running along the floor and ceiling for traveling the circumference of the room, for reaching and dusting.

NUTS was a shrine, an immaculate shop resembling a museum displaying treasured finds. Art cataloged like a repository housing irreplaceably rare books. Hazel was proud of each trifle on display. Thus, the sudden ebb of her clientele – this desertion, evacuation – alarmed her. She stepped out of her high-heeled shoes to climb the rungs of her movable ladder and began dusting the topmost shelf. Positioned to have a better look, an overview of the showroom, she peered about but could not spot a single dust bunny – nor customer– hiding anywhere!

Upon descent, Hazel buffed each rung on the ladder with her fluffy tail. She remounted her shoes and crossed the hardwood floor with her tall heels clicking and her satin dress swishing. Stepping outside, she shook her feather duster, shaking her tail as well. But she stopped in mid-shake. A procession was coming down the street, approaching her doorway. Izzy was in the lead, his ruddy paw gripped to something Hazel had never seen before. Some rarity. A miniature girl. A collectible. Hazel waved her duster as Izzy, who gave a wave back and veered toward her with the little girl in tow.

Izzy squinted. "Hazel!? If you aren't the prettiest feather if ever there was one. You're a sight for poor eyes. Looky here what I got." He released Kat to show her off.

"My, my," said Hazel, clutching the feather duster to her chest.

"I found her," said Wyatt and stepped onto the sidewalk.

"You don't say." Hazel batted her eyes and swished her tail.

Riley flew down, hopping over to Hazel. "Watch yourself! This girl could be dangerous."

"And apparently she's," Izzy said with a yawn, "fully rested."

"Arrested!" Riley bumped Izzy aside.

Izzy pushed Riley back. "What's keep'n Wick?"

"Who cares?" Riley fussed with his cape of black feathers.

"I am *not* dangerous," said Kat. "And it wasn't my idea to wake up in this place. Wherever I am."

"*Oh!*" Hazel was thrilled by this novelty. "She can speak!"

"She sure can," said Izzy, repossessing her arm.

"She's an infiltrator *and* an instigator," said Riley. "Admit it!"

"I am not," said Kat. "I can't even explain *why* I'm here."

"She fell from the sky," said Wyatt, "into Twain River meadow."

"Goodness." Hazel blushed, reminded of her own fall.

Wyatt added, "The same spot you landed, that time I—"

"Need we revisit *that?*" Hazel fanned her face with the duster. She turned to address this rare collectible standing before her. She extended her feathers to lightly dust the top of Kat's head. "Would you like to come inside, miniature girl?"

"Hey!" Kat swiped the duster away. "Don't do that."

"Look at you, you're bleeding." Hazel reached to touch her.

Kat withdrew her arm. "I'm okay."

"She calls herself Kat," said Wyatt. "Kat, this is Hazel."

"Pleased to meet you."

"Cat? How cute. And *pint* size." Unable to constrain herself, Hazel extended the feathers to give Kat another quick dusting.

Kat repelled her head to avoid the feathers. She looked up and noticed the sign hanging above the door. "Nuts?"

Hazel displayed her shiny white teeth. "That's me."

Kat observed the cocktail dress and shoes Hazel was wearing. Around her furry neck hung a gold choker with an emerald pendant in the shape of an acorn. "You look dressed for a fancy party."

"Why, thank you." Enchanted by the compliment, Hazel said, "I so love a good party." Her petite fingers clasped the duster which held her feathers upright like a bouquet of flowers.

"You also look like a squirrel," said Kat.

The bouquet of feathers fell, before transforming back to a fan to supply an ample breeze to her face.

"I didn't... " said Kat. "You *are* a squirrel, aren't you?"

"*Humph.* Miniature girl, learn to have better manners." Hazel turned with a swish of her tail and disappeared inside her shop. The door chimed as she closed it behind her.

A second later, the top portion of her dutch door opened and she poked her head outside. "Well? Are you coming *in* or not?"

Prompted by a push from Izzy, Kat entered Hazel's boutique. Riley squeezed past Wyatt to be next inside after Izzy. Wyatt picked at flecks of paint on his jacket, tightened his cravat, calmed himself with steady intakes of air, then crossed the threshold too, seeking to appear both nonchalant and magnanimous.

"Linger as long as you like." Hazel waved her duster at Kat as if granting a wish from a magic wand. "Take anything. Anything you like. Anything at all."

Kat was puzzled by the collection of items displayed on pedestals and shelves that rose and curved around this circular room. All nuts in every shape, material and size, a whole variety of them, yet none bigger than a coconut nor smaller than a hazelnut.

"Everything in here is..." said Kat. "I mean..."

"Yes?" Hazel fluttered her long lashes.

"Nuts."

Hazel touched her pendant. "What did you expect? There is nothing more worthy than a nut."

"If you're squirrel, I guess. Sorry."

"Don't be," said Hazel. "I feel sorry for *you* – a miniature girl who has fallen from the sky. Take a look around. Go, look around. You will find no nut in here is the same."

Kat looked around to be polite.

Hazel swiveled upon her toes to address her small audience – Wyatt, Riley, Izzy – who were clustered and clogging the entrance to her shop. "Move, move, *move!*" She herded them with her duster, swiping and stirring to make them circulate and clear the front door to collect more customers. "Welcome! Come in. Don't be shy."

A small pigeon carrier swooped down and landed on the bottom half of her dutch door. He wore a blue jacket, short pants and cap. He held out a package.

"Another gift? For me?" So adorable in his uniform, the little bird could be one of her collectibles, thought Hazel wishing to keep him. "Why, thank you. Stay awhile. Don't be shy."

The bluebird tipped his beak at his half-full satchel, then peeped and flew off.

Hazel went back to greeting more customers. "Yes, come in!" She felt renewed that her shop was filling up again. But expressed mild disapproval, pursing her lips and swishing her tail, when she saw everyone's attention was focussed on the miniature girl and not her collection of art. She dusted her way over to Kat.

"Do you have any questions?"

"Lots," said Kat. "Where do you find all of these?"

"I don't. They find me. See?" Hazel unwrapped her package to display the delivery. "Take a peek. See how it feels. Go on."

It was a silvery hickory nut. Kat reached into the box.

"No *touching!*" Hazel chattered a laugh. "I'm teasing. You can touch. Please—*touch.*"

The squirrel appeared to be harmless, so Kat reached back in and lifted the nut out. Its weight surprised her. "Is this real silver?"

"Everything I have is real," said Hazel.

Kat curiously ran her fingertips along the seams of this oblong nut which came to an apex, the remnants of a stem. Like a button. Which she felt compelled to push.

"Oh!" Kat exclaimed.

The nut unhinged, popping open like the wings of a beetle to reveal a sparkling interior – a valley with a gold path traversing the circumference down to a lake of sapphires and diamonds.

"It's so pretty. Are these real jewels?"

"Well why wouldn't they be?"

Kat placed the nut back. "It must be worth a fortune."

"Piffle," said Hazel. "Everything in here is priceless. Worthless though, without its essence."

"Essence?" Kat noticed that everyone was watching her.

"We are lost until our essence is found," said Hazel. "Oh! You must climb the ladder."

"Why?"

"Are you afraid of heights?"

"Not really."

"Then climb! Tell me what you find up there."

Kat grasped the ladder. Each rung and rail was from a branch sanded smooth but still curved and textured. She noted the top and bottom rails were capped with brass rollers and linked to tracks that circumnavigated the interior walls of the tree. She climbed three rungs to be eye level with the second shelf.

"Lots of nuts," she remarked.

"Go all the way up," encouraged Hazel, "to the tippy top!"

Kat became overwhelmed as she climbed past row upon row of shelves displaying nuts that encompassed the room. Blown glass, sculpted metals, carved crystals, emeralds, sapphires, rubies. So many she became dizzy and clung to the rails.

Holding the ladder from below, Hazel said, "To truly know a nut you need to touch it. And be *touched* by it. Keep going. You're almost there."

Kat reached the top shelf, saw more nuts, and turned her head to view the entire showroom. Along the multitude of curving shelves, each nut was immaculate, sparkling and shining. It felt as if she was looking down into a cavern of jewels untouched by time, treasures from an ancient civilization.

"Now hold on tight!" Hazel began to push the ladder.

Kat clutched the rails as glittering nuts passed before her eyes.

Hazel shouted to her, "Tell me when I should—"

"Stop!"

Kat's heart was beating rapidly. She didn't understand why. She loved thrill rides. She climbed all sorts of things – towering oaks and pines, even latticework and vines to climb into bedroom windows. She hopped on and off branches to and from rooftops. This feeling of trepidation was not something she was used to.

"See anyone you like?" said Hazel.

"I don't know." Kat held tight to the ladder.

"For Heaven's sake! You look fixated upon something."

"It's all so…" Kat was lightheaded. "So very…"

"So very what?"

"Shiny. And orderly. You really like to clean."

Hazel stepped away from the ladder. "I *hate* to clean."

"It wasn't meant as an insult," said Kat.

"Oh." Hazel smiled and retrieved her duster placed on a shelf. "Who *will* if I won't? Particles are everywhere. We're composed of particles. They fall from us every single second of every single day. At times I feel the entire world is falling apart. Into these itty-bitty tiny bits and pieces."

Kat had closed her eyes to concentrate on not falling. She was suddenly envisioning the world as one giant dust ball.

"Simply holler when you've found it," said Hazel.

Kat opened her eyes. "Found what?"

"Your nut, silly. Have you been listening to a thing I've said? You'll know it when it speaks to you."

From atop the ladder Kat gazed down upon the circular room filled with animals dressed like humans, their heads raised, their eyes scrutinizing her. The crow had pulled his goggles back to rest on his feathered head while his beady eyes were vigilantly riveted upon her. In sharp contrast, the beaver had fallen asleep leaning against a wall. She located the frog in this crowded showroom. His reassuring smile was somewhat comforting. The squirrel's toothy grin, not so much. She was directly under the ladder.

"What do you mean?" said Kat. "Nuts can't talk."

"Miniature girl," said Hazel. "Don't be a simpleton. *Listen.*"

"To what?"

"Oh, for goodness sake. Why don't you try and pretend you *are* a cat for once. Try that."

"Why?"

"To see the world anew."

"I'd say I am."

"Are you? Really? With *cat* eyes?"

"Okay. Fine. " Kat turned back to face the nuts on the top shelf. The whole place *was* nuts, she decided. Descending the ladder, she reached the floor and looked about, going through the motions of showing interest. She touched a nut on its pedestal, a couple more displayed on shelves, before facing Hazel with a shrug.

"Nope. Nothing. Not a peep."

"Nothing can sometimes be something," said Hazel.

"Maybe they're not talkative today."

Hazel furrowed her furry brow.

As Wyatt approached, Kat said, "He talks to nature."

Wyatt touched his beret. "Ladies."

"Can you tell me which nut here has a *thing* for me?"

Hazel was not amused by Kat's attitude.

"You must be the one who hears it," said Wyatt. He opened his jacket to expose an emerald nut pinned to his vest. Identical to the acorn upon Hazel's choker. "It talks in mysterious ways. You see? One did speak to me. Once upon a time."

Hazel's cheeks flushed. She felt compelled to dust.

Wyatt winked at Kat and playfully pontificated, "Every nut, like us, is unique, with an inner kernel and an outer shell."

"So?" said Kat.

"In a nutshell, we are kings and queens bound in infinite space, searching for our *soul* mate."

Hazel swished back to say, "He's wildly imaginative. But right. Even you, miniature girl, as tiny as you may be, could stand to grow your mind a bit. Even a cat knows it has an *essence*."

"I'm not a *cat*," said Kat.

"Who said you were?" said Hazel.

"Kat is only my *nickname*," said Kat.

Hazel stopped dusting. "Why is your name nicked? How and when did this happen? I detect no *flaw*."

"Spelled with a *K*. Kat is short for Kathlyn."

Hazel continued dusting. "Well that explains nothing."

Kat shook her head in frustration, rapidly blinking her eyes. She did this when arguing with her older brother and sister who could be just as exasperating. This acquired habit surfaced as a nervous tick when she stood before her teachers or parents trying to justify her actions – disrupting class with her jokes, sneaking out her bedroom window at night – which were considered deviations from the norm. Her own behavior she could barely explain to herself sometimes.

"What is that you are doing?" asked Hazel.

"Nothing." Kat realized she had been blinking and stopped, felt foolish and looked around in a daze.

"Well, for heaven's sake, do *something*."

Compelled to act, Kat picked up a random nut. In shape and size, it was an acorn, but made of glass.

"Did you hear it speak?" said Hazel.

"No." Kat held the tiny sculpture up to the light. In its center was a curious speck of gold in the shape of a cube. The glass felt unnaturally warm.

Hazel prodded, "What is it telling you?"

Kat set the nut back on its pedestal. "Not very much."

The acorn wobbled a bit before settling. As Kat turned away, the nut began to meander and roll toward her off the pedestal.

Hearing a unified gasp from those around her, Kat turned and caught the acorn in mid air.

"It obviously likes you," said Hazel.

Kat scoffed. "Why? Because I saved its life?"

"Don't be snippety. You felt something."

"It feels warm, is all." Kat began to put it back.

"You need it. This nut will keep you safe."

Kat pointed to the sides of her dress. "No pockets. I don't have any money. *Sorry*. No sale today."

"Piffle. Nothing here is for sale!" Hazel harrumphed, chattering in a laugh.

"Isn't that a price tag?" Kat indicated a sticker on the pedestal. The numbers were so tiny they were illegible.

"No." Hazel fluttered her eyelashes, amused. "No one can *buy* that kind of value. It's priceless!"

Kat closed her eyes and shook her head, wishing again she could wake from this dream. "If no one can *buy* anything, then what is the point of having a store?"

"To share."

"Are you saying nothing here is for sale?"

"Absolutely *not*." Hazel dusted the top of Kat's head.

"Stop doing that. Everything is free?"

"Miniature girl," said Hazel, "Nothing is *free*."

"This is confusing," said Kat.

"She thinks *I'm* confusing too," said Wyatt. "And *silly*."

"Does she?" Hazel turned to give Kat a playful pout. "It seems that I have underestimated you. Wyatt confuses *me* too."

Kat giggled.

"What a delightful little laugh you have," said Hazel.

Riley had been impatiently mulling about and had heard enough.

"What is so funny? This girl is trouble, Hazel. Has she gone and bewitched you too?"

Hazel sashayed past Riley to shake out her duster through the dutch door. "*Whom* should I believe? You? Someone who cannot for the life of him find his own nut?"

"I have plenty of nuts! I *eat* nuts for breakfast!"

Snoring in a chair, Izzy snorted as Hazel paused to give his head a light dusting. Customers were roaming about, pretending to shop. Others were crowded outside her door. More were gathered in the street. She turned back to Kat. "Where was I?"

"Isn't the point of having a store," said Kat, "to sell things?"

Hazel laughed. "What good could *ever* come of that?" Amused, she set down her duster. On the side of a pedestal she pulled out a drawer and removed a gold chain. "I mean—*really*."

"*Really*," Riley snidely echoed, "did you think *I* was for sale, minuscule girl? Well—I am not!"

Kat backed away from the crow. "I only meant—"

"Now hold *still*." Hazel grasped Kat by her shoulders.

"Come on, Riley," Wyatt joked, "you know you can be bought."

"That is *not* true!" Riley reiterated to Kat. "It is not."

Hazel pulled Kat closer to hang an ornate gold chain around her neck, then held out her gloved hand. "Hand me your nut."

Kat opened her palm.

Through a hole in the crystal acorn Hazel threaded the chain, snapped its clasp, then let the pendant fall, before stepping back to admire her work. She clicked her high heels. "Perfection!"

Kat touched it. "Thank you."

"See, you found your manners too. You are welcome."

Riley stuck his nose between them. "But what about her wrists? Bare. She needs some bracelets."

"You poor thing," said Hazel. "Your skin is all torn. And you've been bleeding. Let me have a look."

Kat held up her wrists. "They're only scratches."

Riley snapped handcuffs on Kat – cuffing both wrists. "There! And look how they match! A perfect *fit*."

"Hey!" cried Kat.

"Caw-ha! Now it's off to jail for you, tiny girl."

Kat was pulled by the crow.

Wyatt hopped in front to block the door. "You can't—"

"Out of my way!" Riley forcefully shoved Wyatt onto the sidewalk where he tripped over bystanders and stumbled, falling onto the cobblestone street. Riley grabbed a silver walnut off a shelf and threw it at Izzy. It bounced off his snoring head. "Wake up! I've got a prisoner!"

"What'd I miss?" Izzy snorted, rubbing his eyes. "What's up?"

"Please," begged Kat, "I just want to go home."

"I have a home for you," said Riley. "It's called a *cage.*"

"Come back!" cried Hazel. "Don't everyone leave at once."

Izzy rose to his feet, taking charge in a fit of confusion. "What'd she do? What did I miss? Who'd she harm?"

Hazel pointed, desperately wanting Kat back. "She–she—"

"*Stole* from ya? Dam thief! Knew it." Izzy dragged his tail over the floorboards and pushed his way out the door and dug his claws into Riley's feathers. "Give 'er back!"

Riley squawked, "Get your own girl!"

Izzy spotted the pendant around Kat's neck. He clamped a paw around it, yanking her by the chain. "You a klepto?"

"A what?" said Kat.

"*Maniac,*" Izzy clarified. "A thief!?"

"No," said Kat. "I didn't take it! She—"

"Looks to me like you *took* it. Ain't wise to take a gift horse outa the house, *iz* it!?" Izzy held tight to the pendant, tugging.

Wyatt was pushing through the crowd circled around Riley and Izzy who were fighting over Kat. "Let her go!"

Hazel cried out, "Be careful not to damage the little girl!"

Kat was being thrust and tugged in opposite directions by her chain and handcuffs. "What do you mean, a gift horse?"

"You heard me!" said Izzy.

"Izzy, let go of the chain!" screeched Riley.

After being pulled this way and that, having come to a standstill, Kat tried to remain calm. She asked the beaver, "Did you mean to say I shouldn't look a gift horse in the mouth?"

Izzy rubbed his whiskers. "No! Don't go mixing up my words. I said what I meant. And what you said makes no *scent* at all. I got a nose for smelling the truth."

"I thought you meant I was being ungrateful."

"Are ya?"

"*No*... I," said Kat, "don't know what to think anymore."

Riley squawked, "She's cracking! See? I'm making progress. Out of my way, Izzy. Let me do my work!"

Izzy released the chain. "Well if rats don't eat all. Take her."

Riley hauled Kat into the street, "You *will* confess or else."

"Or else what?"

"You had wished you *had*." Riley crowed, "Over here, lads!"

The crowd separated and a wagon appeared. It was pulled by four zebras chained together, standing erect, all uniformed in black-and-white stripes. They were shouldering the burden of lugging this four-wheeled contraption over the cobblestones. The wagon held an iron cage. The gang of crows was riding it like armed security.

"See the trouble you've brought on," said Izzy.

"But I didn't do anything," said Kat.

"Then explain to me how ya got here?" said Izzy.

"I can't," said Kat.

"Or *won't*," said Riley.

Izzy told her, "Everything ya do has its cons and penances."

"You mean consequences?" asked Kat.

"Stop chopping up my words!" Izzy scratched at his spiky fur. "Let the chips fall where I say."

A larger crowd had now reassembled around them.

Wyatt fought his way to the center of the commotion. "Help me stop this, Izzy. Before it gets out of control."

"Ya can't stop the unstoppable. The cork is outa the bottle."

"She doesn't deserve this," said Wyatt.

"Let Riley contaminate the situation. He's head of security."

Hazel maneuverered through the horde of busybodies, padding barefoot over the cobblestones with her high-heeled shoes dangling from her gloved paws. "What is all this ruckus?"

Kat was being hoisted in the air by Riley and his cronies. They shoved her into the cage. The door was slammed shut and clamped with a padlock. "There!" Riley turned to Wyatt. "Now we all have ourselves a real *pet*. Who is no longer a *threat*."

"Wyatt," said Hazel, "do something."

"I'll go get Wick," he told her.

"Wick!?" Riley overheard him and squawked a laugh.

"You're wasting your dime," said Izzy.

"But he is our elected leader," said Hazel.

"Who ran unopposed," stated a baboon, scratching his nose.

"Be a hero," Riley mocked. "Go fetch Wick!"

A raccoon, holding a briefcase, said, "What a useless tool."

"And *shifty* as the sand too," hissed a snake.

"Not even a nail gun can pin that weasel down," shouted Izzy.

The horde of animals snorted and hooted with laughter.

"B-b-but he m-means well," bleated a black sheep.

"If he could be counted on," said a chipmunk.

"To hold an opinion," added a possum.

"Cause he ain't got none," said a rat, picking his teeth.

"Or a mind of his own," snarled a cougar.

"And *that* is because," said Camille, breezing through the crowd, her body now a flowing fuchsia, rotating her eyes on the assembled crowd, "Wick is all things to no one. The voice of us all."

Wyatt landed with a hop and clatter on the top of Kat's cage. He tapped his pine-needle stick on the bars and peered down at Kat with a determined smile. "Fear not. I am here to rescue you. I will get you out of this mess."

"Nice job so far," said Kat.

"Relax," he told her. "It's a minor setback. Just a delay."

"Between point A to point B?" said Kat sarcastically.

"I'll be right back. Stay put."

Wyatt sprang off – leaping over the crowd.

Kat felt as helpless as a beetle imprisoned inside a flower. Worse. Everyone could see her. She clutched the bars, exposed on all sides, staring back at the swarm of creatures – mammals, reptiles, insects – there to observe her. She was being displayed like an exotic animal at a zoo. Any moment she thought she might faint.

Her senses were aroused by a familiar face in the crowd. Hazel, waving her duster like a pennant, who was there to cheer her on.

"I don't seem to be very welcome here," said Kat.

"Piffle," said Hazel. "You are a wonder to behold. A rarity. Like a collectible. You should feel honored."

"To be placed inside a cage?"

"And so cute! Henceforth, I shall call you *Kitten*."

"Please don't."

68

chapter five

Harold Hare

Harold Hare was hunched over a leather-bound book, holding a magnifying glass to read the fine print as he scanned the pages. It was one of several law books piled upon his massive, solid-burl executive desk. A stylish desk, adorned with gold-leaf classical moldings and antique brass handles. Its cabriole legs were exquisitely carved. Harold was extremely proud of this piece of furniture, though its beauty was rarely witnessed, for it was habitually covered with precarious stacks of books and folders and binders from which an avalanche of paper spewed forth to hang and inevitably fall off its rococo ledges. Harold was hard at work on writing a document, a theory he was in the process of formulating. The gist of his treaty was derived from case studies on marriage and divorce, including his own personal history – which was extensive – on the subject of matrimony and extramarital affairs. Harold was an attorney. He practiced Family Law. Which meant he dealt with the contractual Mr. and Mrs. (an X versus Y) who encountered the inevitable stages of attraction, fixation, attrition and repulsion. A predictable sequence of events that never failed to fail. Therefore, Harold (aka *Harry* – a moniker he detested yet persistently haunted him like the many close encounters he'd had with the female kind) succinctly summarized the results of his research as such:

Love was messy.

Harold stretched back, reclining in his chair, rubbed his pink eyes and pondered the cavernous ceiling. He treated his floppy ears to a brisk scratch before brushing them back. They fell to opposite sides of his head as he stood and consulted his timepiece, a brass antique pocket watch he had inherited from the generations of Hares. He popped open the cover. Both the short and long hands were attached at the hub, but hung limply, pendulously pointing to 6. No change. Harold had come to believe that with regard to time, it was not the precision nor duration of time that mattered — it was the routine of one's practices. Clicking his pocket watch shut, he began wondering whether it was too early to resurface for another meal. He guessed it was close to either brunch or lunch. Having plenty of time to squander, Harold indulged himself by wasting as much time as was possible. There were plenty of underlings capable of operating the mechanisms of Hare & Heirs, the family law practice which he had been born into and now over-efficiently run by many offspring from countless couplings.

Admittedly, mathematics left him cold. Nor was he fond of the counting game – keeping track of the number of lovers he had *had*. Suffice it to say, there had been many. Yet Scarlet was the dominate figure of late. A major player and by far the majority stockholder in his mind. He could think of nothing else. He glanced at his messy desk and had a fleeting thought to straighten it before looking down at the plush red carpet which made him think of Scarlet. He kicked aside fallen papers with his big furry foot to see more of its swirling pattern which stirred his mind to envision more of her. He popped open his watch to shake the hands of time. This anticipation – this longing to see her again – was killing him. He wet the pink pads of his hands, smoothed his scruffy eyebrows, then combed his floppy ears to try and straighten and coax them upwards into proper points. But they refused to stay aloft and fell to his sides. It had become a ritual, trying to commit his ears to remain upright. Also a ritual to abandon the idea in frustration. He was interrupted by a thought – a roving reminder to grab his tiny notebook buried under his pile of papers. He looked down at his large feet and wiggled them. Which made him wistful, mindful of the firm grip he no longer had upon the threshold of love.

Yet with Scarlet's help he had reclaimed his virility.

On his way to the door he checked himself – padding waistcoat, pants, and bowtie – to make sure he was all there and fully dressed. He appeared to be, yet was wearing the same three-piece grey suit from the day before which he had slept in upon his leather couch.

He ventured out the door to plunge into a stream of energetic bunnies moving frenetically fast with their quick greetings:

"Good morning, Father."

"A meeting a two, Harold, don't forget."

"Hi, Dad."

"Another long night, Harry?"

"Hello, Father."

With vacant nods, Harold acknowledged each worker he passed on his journey through the passageways of Hare & Heirs Enterprise. The Rules of Proper Conduct were paramount to Harold. Though broadly-based and debatable, he believed they were something akin to sacred tablets one had to swallow. Metaphorically, that is. Rules mattered. Customs mattered. Good judgement mattered. He knew all this. But Scarlet, she was an entirely different matter. She was an exception to all these rules.

He made a passing glance at a wall mural – saw a flicker of red – and imagined Scarlet again. Her face. His mind went elsewhere, no longer bound to the constraints of business nor confined to these interconnecting tunnels. So, instead of his usual short cut, he took a long cut, venturing down a recently completed passageway to waste more time. He found himself pondering the many murals exhibiting vistas of unfamiliar places, yet destinations he felt he should know.

Did these locations even exist?

Having turned a corner, Harold stopped to scratch his ears. He backed away from an enormous pane of glass to take in the breadth of this wall-to-wall and floor-to-ceiling window view of the exterior. Yet there was none. They were underground. The interior space had a large pond and fountain in its center. He looked back at the mural depicting glass. It darkly foreshadowed glimmers of water and light. He realized the mural was a reflection of the room. He glanced back and forth, at the pond and the painting, detecting ghostlike figures –

who were not obvious at first – peering inside! As if into a mirror!
Standing on the other side of a looking glass!

Harold shuddered with intrigue at the discovery, by this trick of
perspective. He was provoked. What did it mean? Stepping closer,
he noticed how the brushstrokes of colors were feathered, merging,
absorbed and disappearing into swirls of black ink. These gigantic
figures were noticeable only from a distance. And even then, barely.
He detected scribbling along the bottom at the other end of the wall.
Someone had taken credit for this ineffable aberration:

Wyatt T. Frog.

The name meant nothing. But Harold, unabashedly, was not
good with names. He recalled very few. With the exception of one.
Scarlet Fox. Her name sent waves of tingling pleasure to every fur
follicle in his body. He snapped open his timepiece to confirm it was
still six-thirty. Time had stopped. It felt reassuring. He deposited
the worthless piece of gears back into his vest pocket and departed
down another hallway, moving faster now.

He continued to nod at the passing faces, many his progeny.

He stopped to insert his head into the main library to see a game
of cards in progress, but he declined the summons by his colleagues
to partake in their poker game. He gestured heartily, indicating a
prior commitment. Which was untrue. But who among them could
fault his passion to seek and conquer the heart of Scarlet?

If they only knew her like he knew her.

Money mattered. But hearts trumped diamonds. Always.

Harold dashed off to catch an elevator in the maze of hallways,
squeezing inside the box, taking up space within a horde of others.
The steel container rose and delivered them to ground level. Harold
emerged near the subway station, near central park and main street.
From a manicured lawn adorned with gravel paths and flower beds
he would situate himself in one of the public benches to have a direct
view of the storefronts circling the town square, yet aimed at one in

particular, at a wall of ivy adorned with a sign:

The Outside-In Palace.

Harold drifted, as if in a spell, upon his large feet, stopping to consult his pocket watch (prop that it was), and gave it a dignified nod as if to confirm the time (six-thirty), brushed back his ears, then found the proper bench to place his buns on (same bench, each day, every time) until finding courage to cross the street and face Scarlet, who operated the Outside-In Palace. His palms had begun to sweat and his underarms were as soggy as swamps. As well, he felt the beads of perspiration now collecting in the nests of his eyebrows. Surreptitiously, he gave them a swipe, expelling water to prevent any precipitation. He mentally fought to quell his anxiety and pacify his nerves but nothing seemed to work. It was befuddling.

He was never nervous when confronting an opponent in court. Instead, he was known for his steadfast nerves – *unnerving* his rivals. Confidence was his trademark. And his claim to fame – presenting a calm demeanor when arguing a case and claiming victory. Anxiety, he acknowledged, was a natural reaction with most confrontations. The trick was rechanneling energy. But this was different. Absurd! Harold rubbed his palms upon his legs in an effort to keep them dry. The rigorous friction caused another unpredictable phenomenon to occur. Without needing to reach up and verify by touching, Harold knew his ears were standing perfectly erect. As if at attention! Alert. What source, other than Scarlet, could he attribute this rechanneling of his blood flow? None. Was this passionate surge apparent to all? He shifted his bottom on the bench. His fingers toyed with the chain spanning a coat button to the bulge in his pocket. He was tempted to consult his timepiece, yet opted not to look, although imagining what he would see – the tiny hands pointing straight up!

12:00! Post Meridiem! High noon!

Had the magnetic poles shifted?

Had the world turned upside down?

Indeed, the world *had*, thought Harold. For when he looked up, he saw a tiny girl inside a cage! She was no bigger than all the rest of them. The crow, beaver, squirrel – all parading down the center of town with her in tow as if the End of Days was near!

Harold stood, incensed by the presumed injustice taking place, and leaped forward to intercede this mob. He officiously blocked their passage with the only tool he had to justify his actions. From his coat pocket he withdrew the container holding his business cards. It was razor thin and as bright as a lodestar. It caught the sunlight.

"What is the meaning of this outrage!?"

Riley shielded his eyes. "Drop your weapon!"

Harold ignored him and walked right up to the circus-wagon jail to ask the little girl, "Have they harmed you in any way?"

Kat blinked, peering out, "I don't think so."

"Do you have legal representation?"

"I don't know."

"My card." Harold handed it to her handcuffed hands through the bars. "Take it. I am an attorney!"

Kat took the card.

"I happen to be the best."

"Do I need an attorney?" said Kat.

"Are you joking? *Everyone* needs an attorney."

"But why?"

"Why? Look at you!"

"I'm innocent," said Kat. "I didn't do anything."

"Exactly," said Harold. "That is how the law works."

"*Harry*," said Hazel, "For heaven's sake, why are you scaring this poor thing? She's scared enough already."

Harold cringed at the use of his pet name, yet gave her a brief smile of acknowledgement, before focusing back on Kat. "Everyone needs legal representation."

Riley flipped back his goggles to squawk. "Go away! No one

needs you – Hare & Heirs!"

"Are you responsible for this?" said Harold.

Riley gave a noncommittal scowl.

"Your actions are unconstitutional," Harold added.

"Homeland security!" stated Riley. "Heard of it?"

Harold scratched his whiskers, took out his note pad and began scribbling notes. "On what grounds—"

"*My* grounds," said Riley.

"Twain River meadow," explained Hazel. "Wyatt was the one who found her."

"Wyatt, you say?" asked Harold.

"He saw her fall from the sky," said Hazel.

"Who fell from the sky?"

"Kat," said Hazel. "This miniature girl."

"Who's a cat?"

"She ain't no cat," said Izzy.

"She calls herself that," said Hazel.

"My *name* is Kat," said Kat.

"What? No—no—no." Harold was crossing out words from his notes and roared. "Inadmissible! You can't incarcerate someone for thinking they're a cat!"

"I can arrest and imprison whomever I please," said Riley.

"You have no legal authority to incarcerate a cat," said Harold, handing Kat another card. "You've been treated unjustly. I'm here to champion your cause and set you free."

"Thank you," said Kat.

"Wait to you get a load of his *unjustified* fee," said Riley.

"Inadmissible," said Harold. "Have you been read your rights?

"I don't believe so," said Kat.

"Say no more!" said Harold.

"Harry," said Hazel, "the little girl is only lost."

"And," stated Harold, poking Kat through the bars, attempting to tickle her chin. "A rather *defenseless* one, I would say."

Izzy squinted at Harold. "Look. Ya got 'ur ears *fixed*."

Harold turned to defend his left flank, informing Izzy. "My ears were never broken!"

A sultry voice said, "Harry has *adorable* ears."

Harold flinched – feeling his ears being touched – and turned to see Scarlet. Her presence left him speechless, sputtering nonsensical syllables into the air, and coming up short of a full smile. His cheeks were turning red. His pinks nose began to twitch.

Scarlet Fox was indeed a fox.

And in Harold's totally biased opinion she was the embodiment of unadulterated beauty. She had pert little ears. Her face was sleek and soft, the perfect blend of reddish brown and white fur. Her nose tapered to a petite point. And the combination of her mouth (which harbored thin but luscious lips) along with her cosmetic eyes (both lids lined with black accents) formed a magnetic triangulation of wildly mysterious waters where all bets were off.

Riley too was entranced and flared his brows and extended his winged cape to magnanimously present Kat. "Look what I captured, Scarlet. I caught her crossing the bridge into Evolsdog. She's quite the catch, is she not?"

Harold was rebuilding his confidence, straightening his bowtie.

"Wick is on his way," said Hazel, "to voice *his* opinion."

Harold spun at her. "Wick? Wick has no opinion. His decisions are based on straw polls, conducted by sycophants on halfhearted participants who do the surveys to amuse him but could care less. Convict this girl based on that weasel's obtuse judgement? The trial would be travesty of justice! A farce! I won't allow it! I will *not*." He glanced at Scarlet with a look of judicious assurance, followed by a stately wink.

"Who said anything about having a trial?" said Riley.

"There *has* to be a trial," said Harold. "That's the law."

"Please tell me what I've done wrong," said Kat.

"Let *me* determine that." Harold began doodling copious notes into his tiny book. "I will need to interview this... *Wyatt* character. As to what he might have seen. Does anybody know him?"

"Yes," said Hazel, "And so do *you*, Harry."

"Hum. Perhaps I do. Do I?"

Harold tore out a slip of paper from his notebook, crumpled, then tossed it to the ground. A pigeon scurried over to sweep and scoop it up with a broom into a dustbin.

"Now," continued Harold, "for the record, what is the specific grievance leveled against my client. By the plaintiff? Defendant? Anyone?"

"I would like to go home," said Kat from her cage.

Harold ripped out another page and crumpled it into a ball. He tossed it to the cobblestones with righteous disgust. "I *too* would like to go home. We *all* would like that, insignificant girl."

"Kat," said Kat.

"What's that?" said Harold.

"*Harry*," said Hazel, "she calls herself Kat."

Harold's left eye began to twitch. "Let's not complicate matters by using *pet* names. Let's maintain a modicum of professionalism."

"I *was* serious." Hazel bared her teeth in a barely civil smile.

Harold touched pen to his tongue. "Seriously?"

"*Seriously*," said Kat, "It's short for Kathlyn."

"What is?"

"My name," said Kat. "It's Kat. But spelled—"

"Ah-ha! *But!*" Harold held up a furry finger to silence her. He wrote furiously. "The use of the word 'but' implies you are hiding a *lie* somewhere. What? Where is it? Speak up, little girl."

"Mr. Rabbit. My nickname *is* Kat. But I am *not* a cat! Please, will someone let me out of here?"

Harold touched pen to tongue again. "Hum, I do detect a feline resemblance. You may *be* a cat. Have you considered that?"

"No! Because I'm a *girl*. A human."

"But you called me a *rabbit*."

"Aren't you?"

"I happen to be a *hare*."

"Isn't that the same thing?"

"Proportionally, no," said Harold. "Are you really a girl?"

"Yes," said Kat.

"Aren't girls proportionally larger than rabbits and hares?"

"Normally."

"*Normally...* ah-ha!" Harold jotted more notes.

"I meant, usually," said Kat.

"Except not *today*? Is that what you're saying?"

"Well, yes, not *here* anyway," said Kat.

"If not *here*," said Harold pointedly, "then *where*? And *how* do I know there was ever a *when* you were ever *there*? And *why* should I believe such a tall tale? *How* can anyone trust anything you say?" Harold tore out more pages, crumpling, tossing them like birdseed. Several pigeons had gathered and were waiting to scoop them up. "*What* was that you said?"

"I didn't say anything," said Kat.

"Well *that* will not help your case," said Harold.

"I wasn't lying. I have no reason to lie."

"Everyone has a reason to lie," said Harold.

"Oh, she *lies*, I caught her in several," said Riley. His booted heals clicked upon the cobblestones. "Where is she from? The sky? What comes from the sky? Aliens! Subversives! Danger! Now, if she *admitted* she was a cat – disguised as a little *brat* – now I might believe that. But no, she's a little girl who fell from the sky! Or so she says. Or so says Wyatt."

Harold scratched his nose. "Who *is* this Wyatt?"

"You know him," said Hazel.

"I do not," said Harold.

"Sure you do," said Izzy.

"Harry's forgetful," said Scarlet.

"I am *not*," said Harold. "Let's keep this professional."

"Will someone please let me out?" pleaded Kat. "I'm not here to harm anyone. I'm telling the truth, I swear!"

"*Pshaw!*" Riley spat into a convenient flower bed. "What kinda world would *that* be if everyone went around telling the truth? We'd all be hating the sight of each other."

"You want me to lie?" said Kat. "Fine—I'm a *cat*. Satisfied?"

"Egad, now you've done it!" Harold snapped shut his notebook and shook his head. He noticed Scarlet. Her eyelids were squinted and her lips pursed, expressing displeasure about something. About him. Her lovely eyes had turned away from him like a juror whose verdict he had lost to the other side. Harold felt his ears go limp.

Kat pointed. "Your ears."

Harold brushed them back. "What *about* them?"

"They… well," she said, "fell down. Apart."

"Like your *alibi*." Harold crumbled another page of his notes. "I highly advise that you to say *nothing* further until you've spoken with an attorney."

"I thought you were an attorney," said Kat.

"Did you wish to hire me?"

"I would if I—"

"Were innocent? Not inane? *Out* with it," coaxed Harold.

"Had money to hire you," said Kat.

"Oh—*swell*," Harold groused. He tucked his book back into his pocket and scratched his ears. "Another charity case. Pro *bono!*" He spun around on the heels of his big feet, critically casting his eyes upon Izzy ensconced upon a park bench snoring vociferously.

"*Harry*," said Scarlet.

Harold spun back like the needle on a compass to face north.

"I do realize this is not my field of expertise. And I am not one to meddle in your *affairs*. But might I offer a suggestion?"

He was all ears. "Scarlet, yes, yes, by all means."

"A short recess?" She winked flirtatiously.

Harold sensed his ears stiffen and rise. His nose began to twitch. "A recess? Yes, let us adjourn! To where?"

Scarlet approached the cage, "Little cat, have they fed you yet?"

Kat had to wonder. "I should be hungry, shouldn't I?"

"See?" Riley pointed. "She admits to knowing *nothing*."

"Now *Riley*," teased Scarlet, "You bad boy. Come over here."

Riley nudged Harold aside. "How might I be of service?"

"You can let her out. For me? Can't you?"

"But... Scarlet. I just got her *in* there."

"Look how uncomfortable she is."

"I'm not in the hospitality business." Riley stuck his beak to the cage. "I enforce the *law*. Did you want a pillow?"

"No, thank you," said Kat.

"Look at her," said Scarlet, "So *petite*. And polite."

"It's a ruse," said Riley.

"*Riley*," snapped Scarlet with a coquettish squint.

"*Scarlet*." Riley whispered, "I have a reputation to uphold."

"For me? Pretty please?"

"This girl is *trouble*," muttered Riley. "Wyatt wanted to keep her as a pet too. And let her run free!"

"You still have her handcuffed," huffed Hazel.

"A big crow like *you*," teased Scarlet, stroking his winged cape, "with all your military might. You can contain a small disturbance like *her*. Can't you?"

Riley felt his masculinity put on the spot, called into question. Refusing Scarlet would imply impotence. Her magnetic attraction was disorienting. All he could think to say was, "You *owe* me."

"Of course I do," she said. "Now let the poor thing out."

Riley grudgingly hopped onto the platform, unclasped the lock with his key, and swung the cage open. Kat emerged with her hands bound, glancing about before jumping down to the cobblestones.

Scarlet extended her bejeweled paw. "Come with me."

Kat lifted her cuffed hands, "Where are we going?"

Scarlet looked at Riley. "Are these really necessary?"

He nodded, not willing to budge this time.

Scarlet took hold of the chain connecting Kat's handcuffs and pulled her along. They had a mass of followers as they crossed the town square to a row of shops. Riley scuttled alongside, slightly in front, keeping his eyes on anyone who came too close, glancing furtively this way and that, waving his wings to clear a path.

They came to a row of storefronts. Stepping onto the sidewalk, Kat saw a flagstone path that meandered into an alleyway, ending at an enormous wall of ivy.

"This is my place," said Scarlet.

There was only ivy and a sign:

OUTSIDE-IN PALACE

There was no discernable doorway, only a solid mesh of ivy.

"Go on in," prodded Scarlet.

"What am I supposed to do?"

"Enter."

"There's no door."

"You squeeze inside," Scarlet told her.

"Squeeze?"

"The foliage will either accept or reject you."

"I don't understand," said Kat.

"It sentient." She indirectly directed her words at Riley. "Much more effective at keeping the riffraff and troublemakers out than any padlock. Go! Inside. Before it gets too late."

"Too late for what?" asked Kat.

"Don't hesitate," said Scarlet. "It will sense your fear."

"It?"

"After the initial shock, it will feel fun."

"What kind of shock?"

"To have fun requires an element of shock."

Kat stepped forward. Behind the towering wall of ivy she could see portions of a glass structure in the blue sky. As she touched the ivy she let out a shriek and was sucked inside.

"So trusting." Scarlet laughed. "Foolish little cat."

chapter six

Wick Weasel

Wick was a weasel. Everyone knew he was. Yet the inhabitants of Evolsdog accepted his obsequiously-egotistical mannerisms and motives and political ambitions because he was good-natured, always on the move, wringing his hands and shaking other hands, constantly darting his long snout left and right as if on the scent for a new vote. As the Prime Minister he was eager to please, if only for show. He was leery of everyone and viewed his constituents as potential rivals, as challengers who wished to unseat him from his seat of power. Which was pure illusion on his part. He had no real power. And no one wanted his job.

Wick had been sworn into office as Sedwick Esquire Burr III. A name no one recognized. Everyone called him Wick and knew him by that name. Being the Prime Minister made him a popular figure. Which he liked – being popular. Likewise, he disliked being called a weasel. It felt unpopular. Epithetic.

A weasel, by implication, was someone who had a reputation of backing out of situations and commitments in a sneaky or cowardly fashion. So, to dispel this myth, Wick made public appearances to appear just the opposite, presiding at holiday parades, fundraising events, baby showers. He made speeches in parks and town halls, and at graduations, anywhere he could speak into a microphone. He loved hearing the sound of his amplified voice.

He kept his whiskers neatly trimmed. Each article of clothing was impeccable, of the finest quality, tailored to flatter his elongated torso and short legs. His quick smile and dashing wit won hearts and indecisive minds. When The Reverend Darryl Puma, his oldest friend, was recently interviewed by a reporter and asked about the Prime Minister's tendencies to equivocate on matters of importance, the Reverend laughed augustly and stated, "Ah, yes, *well*... And I propose, if ever there was a debate on *Creation*, I can assure you Wick would find a way to suck the yolk out of the topic just like an egg and manage to leave an inert shell with the image of *God* intact, with everyone pleasantly scratching their heads."

Wick was tickled by this quote and was squirming pleasurably in the nest of his cotton blankets and silk sheets, unwilling to rise and get dressed. The morning newspaper had arrived tightly rolled upon a tray with his continental breakfast of coffee, fruit and cereal – with the pages now strewn like autumn leaves over the undulating hills of bedding. He was drifting into the warm waters of unconsciousness, submerging into a wet dream, when the commotion outside roused him awake.

Sunshine had filled the room. He scratched sleep from his eyes, sat up, set his feet on the floor and slipped into his slippers. Finding his spectacles on the night stand and attaching them behind his ears, he slowly stood, establishing balance, before shuffling in his pajamas to pull back the curtains and peer out the window.

He was alarmed to see a crowd assembled in town square.

Disturbances of any kind disturbed him.

Next came a rapping at his door which caused his heart to skip to a faster beat – towards panic.

"Yes? Who is it?"

"It's me, Sir. There is a frog at the front door."

"A frog?"

"A frog."

"What does he want?"

"You."

"Why me?"

"It's something urgent, he says."

"Tell him... I'm away... on diplomatic matters."

"He knows you are here, Sir."

"How?"

"You... well, you hardly ever leave the mansion."

"Is it that obvious? Then tell him..."

"Sir?"

"To wait in the parlor while I get dressed—no!"

"No?"

"Tell him... I'm at work in my study. I'll be down soon."

"And for him to wait in the parlor?"

"What? Yes. Tell him that."

Wick listened to the footfalls of his personal assistant descending the stairs, leaving him in silence except for the half-muted persistent commotion rising from the streets.

Wick saw his reflection in the window. He too saw a weasel. There were moments when he was so appalled by his own self image he stuck out his tongue in infantile disgust (as he was now) followed by a shrug – accepting the cards the good lord had dealt him.

To mentally prepare himself for the day he bent over, touching his toes to begin his aerobics – jumping jacks, then running in place. He stopped to rest and pant, then plop down into a lotus position. He closed his eyes to pacify his mind but every nerve in his body was firing signals back and forth from stern to bow – as if he was some ship at war with itself. He was on the verge of declaring defeat. But, as a last resort, he employed a mind-over-matter technique, a proven aid to control his nerves by personifying them into a soothing image. He envisioned Koi fish in a pond. Momentarily soothing him until the swirl of carp transformed into a swarm of rambunctious kittens he could not contain nor herd. Groaning at the transmogrification he succumbed to falling flat on his face. It was an act of submission. On his stomach he proceeded to grunt, hiss, whine, stretch and roll, bending backwards like a bow with no arrow.

In this cobra position, Wick began counting to ten but his resolve uncoiled at three and he snapped back, falling forward on the matt, where he lay in defeat with his body exuding sweat and his nerves feeling burned and frayed.

He got to his feet and hung his head, critically examining the flab accumulating at his midsection. He went to attend to his personal hygiene in the bathroom. It was imperative, he believed, that public figures be groomed and cleansed when facing a crowd. He unlocked a sliding panel on the wall with a key he kept hidden beneath the counter. He pushed aside the shelving which held his toothpaste and other sundries. The shelf slid away to reveal a wall mirror. In which he sheepishly peered into, consulting his image, knowing better than to trust what he saw. These reflections were known to deceive. They never reflected an accurate portrayal of what the viewer had in mind, or imagined themselves to be.

Wick acknowledged his face with a critical gaze before turning the faucet and pouring water into the sink. He splashed, brushed, and gargled his face, teeth, and mouth in a series of noisy grunts, hisses and moans. He concluded by spitting. The finalé. Which was then followed by an encore. A smile. He rehearsed it each morning. It radiated goodwill and displayed confidence. It was to camouflage his true feelings that bordered on sheer panic whenever facing the unknown – *others* – every day.

His smile vanished as he recalled the reason why these looking glasses had been banished. The cause of madness. Disappearances. Not to mention the metamorphosis. He slid back the shelf, locking away the mirror, hiding the key, rushing to get dressed, remembering he had a visitor downstairs.

He became lost inside his walk-in closet by the multitude of choices. He stood staring at the row of suits, all in shades of blue, grey or brown. He selected a light brown suit, grabbed a dark grey suit, but placed both back, compromising on a neutral blue suit. After donning a white shirt, buttoning it down, he selected a tie with proportionately-uniformed green and silver stripes and knotted it around his neck. Wick then embellished his jacket by fastening gold epaulettes to each shoulder and pinning his breast pocket with a medallion – an award he had awarded to himself.

He now felt more dignified and authorized to govern.

At his bedroom door Wick paused to face himself one last time before venturing outside. He unlocked a drawer in which he kept a hand mirror. With a guilty look (since mirrors were contraband) he practiced his winning smile until he felt he perfected the expression. He locked the mirror away, justifying the need for this illegal item as his right – given the pressures that came with being a public servant. In a similar fashion, this was how he justified his many pay raises, tax shelters and extravagant lifestyle. Given the authority to govern, to preserve and uphold the law, placed him in a position that was slightly above the law, he rationalized.

Pacing in his parlor was a bohemian-looking frog, noticeable as such by his black-velvet jacket (bespecked with colors) and a beret – which he removed from his head as Wick entered.

"Wick," said Wyatt, moving quickly toward him.

As a reflex, Wick extended his arm to keep his guest from getting any closer by shaking hands. This formality of having to touch his constituents was something he disliked (not knowing where those clenched digits had been prior to touching *his*) yet he dutifully accepted this ritual as part and parcel of the office he held.

"What seems to be the urgent matter?"

"A little girl," said Wyatt. "She fell from the sky."

"Excuse me?" Wick dismissed it prematurely as a joke. He was prepared to laugh if the moment called for laughter. He half-smiled to prevent becoming the butt of another prank. "Are you joking?"

"Not at all," said Wyatt. "Come see for yourself."

"Must I?"

"Yes. It's important. We need your opinion."

"We?"

"The entire town," explained Wyatt.

"Now?"

"*Now*. Please, let's hurry."

Wick's short fingers diddled at his buttons and his long tail swept the floor as he determined his options. Did he have any other ones? Concluding he had few to none, he said, "Let me get my hat."

An overly-attentive subservient groundhog dressed even sharper than Wick in a canary-yellow three-piece silk suit was there to hand Wick his top hat. He was Wick's personal assistant, speech writer, public relations manager, head chef and butler.

"Thank you, Damian."

"My pleasure, Wick—" Damian slapped his face "—*Sir*. Mr. Prime Minister."

Wishing for a mirror, Wick adjusted the hat on his head by feel, discreetly rubbing the top of this formal headgear. A gesture meant to bring him good luck. One of many superstitions he adhered to. Lastly, he selected a cane with an ornately-carved wooden club (to clench) and a solid metal shaft (to swing). To serve as a means of defense, if needed.

"Okay, I am ready. Shall we be off?"

Wick dreaded stepping outside to enter this swarm of citizenry stirred into a frenzy, voicing complaints to execute their civil rights. He lifted his chin and straightened his long torso to stand erect, to show his good posture. With a reassuring smile he waved his short arms in an attempt to calm everyone. He passed them like a show boat in a grand parade through turbulent waters. His entourage of Damian and Wyatt provided about as much protection as bumpers attached to his starboard and lee railings.

An anonymous someone-in-the-crowd came up and breached his personal space by grabbing his coat, saying, "Have you seen her?" He had no choice but to let himself be touched. He understood the voter's needs. At least he made an effort to pretend he did.

"Who?" said Wick.

"The little girl!"

"She's the same size as us!"

"Why is she here?"

"Some say she entered through a mirror."

"Through a mirror!?" Wick began to perspire.

"She didn't," said Wyatt. "She fell out of the sky."

"Wick, that's not right."

"Make her leave!"

"Everyone," said Wick, pummeled by a barrage of questions and concerns. "Calm down. Everything will be explained in due time."

"How?"

"In what way?"

"Wick, explain. How can she remain that way?"

"Maybe the professor is testing us."

"One of his new puzzles?"

"To be included for tonight's entertainment?"

"Will there be a trial?"

Wick stopped to stare at his assistant. "A trial? Perhaps, if..."

Damian took the cue. "Leave it to me, Sir."

"Do we accept her as she is?"

"She has to change."

"Wick, this is unorthodox."

"It's against the constitutional rules."

"It is, isn't it?"

"Wick, what's your opinion?"

"Well..." Wick had to stop and think. Multi-tasking was not his strong suit. Having to think on his feet was hard enough. Mobility made it worse, overtaxing his brain and making it stall. "I... I will have an *opinion* once I have seen this little girl."

"After you talk with her?"

Wick stopped again. "She can talk?"

"Yes, she can," said Wyatt.

"I heard her!"

"It's truc!"

"Like us!"

Wick's intrigue was piqued, causing a minute tremor of nerves. He smiled too broadly, venturing on again, clicking the metal tip of his cane to guide him across the cobblestones. "Where is she?"

"Riley locked her in a cage," said Wyatt.

"In a cage!?" said Wick. "Is she dangerous?"

A mole shouted, "They let her out!"

Wick tried to curb his alarm. "B-but—*why?* Who—"

Wyatt told him, "She did nothing wrong! That's why. And she was imprisoned unjustly. Where is she now?"

"In the Outside-In Palace," said a sloth.

Wick had to stop again. "Outside the... in the—what?"

"Scarlet's place," said Damian.

"Who?" Wick frowned before becoming mobile again.

The crowd began to part as they walked into a narrow alleyway. The weasel found himself face to face with a blockade of crows.

"Step aside," said Wick.

The crows were unmoving.

"I said *excuse* me." Wick brandished his cane. "I need to enter."

The crows had formed a solid barricade.

"You heard him," said Wyatt. "Move aside!"

"No," said one of the crows.

"Do you realize who this is?" said Damian.

"*Who?*" said a crow on the far end.

The crows could barely contain straight faces.

"The *Prime Minister*—that's who!" shouted Wick.

"I will check with my boss."

The crow who spoke backed out of the line, spun around, then disappeared into the foliage by touching it. The other crows moved together to fill in the gap.

Wick tapped his cane and fumed, "I–am–your–boss!"

"No. You are the *Prime Minister*, you said."

The crows began to snigger.

Wick looked at Wyatt. "I cannot tolerate insubordination."

"Then you won't like Riley," said Wyatt.

"Who?"

"Head of security," said Wyatt. "You appointed him."

"I certainly did *not*," said Wick. "I don't... do I even know—"

Damian whispered, "He volunteered, Sir. To be self-appointed. You rubber-stamped the paperwork."

"I did?" Wick glared back at his assistant. "Take a note. I want this crow's post *terminated* immediately, once we—"

"You can't," said Wyatt.

"I *can* too," said Wick. "Why can't I?"

His assistant informed him, "He included a clause granting the Department of Homeland Security independent, judicially, from the other branches of government. Which means he overrules you."

Wick clenched the ball of his cane. "Why that is *absurd!*"

"We agree," said Wyatt. "We watched you sign it into law."

Wick had begun to perspire and removed his hat. "That leaves me rather... I mean, rather... powerless against this—this—"

"We have other means at our disposal," said Wyatt.

Wick squinted through his glasses. "Who are you, again?"

"Wyatt T. Frog."

"Make a note to *award* this fellow a medal of honor."

"We gave out all our medals, Sir," said Damian.

"A blue ribbon, a red token—*something*," hissed Wick.

Their attention shifted to the wall of ivy. It began to stir. Riley materialized from its center to preside among the barricade of crows. Riley was quicker than Wick and spoke first.

"Who invited you?"

"How *dare* you." Wick swept his arms toward his constituents. "I am the Prime Minister! *They* asked me to come here!"

Riley regarded the assembled mob. With a curt bow to mock his allegiance, he said, "Very well. After you, your *Highness*."

Wick grunted and walked through the line of crows.

The gap closed to stop Wyatt and Damian from passing.

"This doesn't concern you or *you*," said Riley.

Wick turned and barked, "They will be coming too!"

Riley refused to budge, then relented. He squawked at his gang of crows. "No one else! Crowd control! Enforce it!"

Wick hesitated at the ivy wall, not sure what to do. Wyatt came up from behind and pushed him into the foliage, transporting them both to the opposite side. Damian followed. Where all three found themselves standing in a foyer and staring into a multitude of eyes belonging to the bearded face of a spider. The majority of its legs and arms were extended, eight in all, touching the walls and floor of this small enclosure. The middle two arms were crossed in front, resting upon a stone edifice.

"Do you have a reservation?"

Wick was discombobulated. Not only by this spider's fibrous body and ball-bearing eyes but by the foyer walls elaborately draped in an enclosure of intricate flowing silk. The ceiling was rib-vaulted. Elaborately-crafted curtains hung from the back wall as if staged for a theatrical production. Enveloped in this white silken ambience, Wick lost his bearings, had no means to navigate by dead-reckoning, having lost all points of reference. Panic set in.

The glittering spider reiterated, "*Reservation?*"

Wick sputtered, "Why... no, I... we. Is one really necessary?"

"No. Only if one wishes to enter."

Wick felt light-headed. The spider's glittering complex of eyes formed a constellation. They felt magnetic. He had to force his eyes away and summon help from Wyatt who seemed equally bedazzled, but who stepped forward to say, "Scarlet knows us."

"Ah... yes. I see. But *I* do not."

"I'm the painter. The mural artist? Wyatt T. Frog. And *this* is the Prime Minister."

"You don't say?" said the officious spider.

"I do say!" To express his irritation Wick had to stare again into these magnetic eyes. Unable to hold his stare, he blinked, trying for more civility. "Sir, or Mister *maître d'*, I am here on urgent matters. To observe the little girl who fell from the sky."

"*Madam.*"

"Excuse me?"

"I am Madam Z. Do I resemble to you a sir… *Sir?*"

Wick blushed. "My apologies."

"Accepted."

Wick removed his hat to wipe his forehead. "Where were we?"

"Do you wish to make a reservation?"

"Now see here!" Wick's outrage was curtailed by the touch of Wyatt's nobby fingers on his shoulder.

"Allow me," said Wyatt calmly. "We would. Yes."

"For how many?"

Madam Z arched her many eyebrows.

Wyatt held up his fingers. "Three."

Wick was losing patience with this supercilious gatekeeper.

"And for what time?"

"*Now!*" Wick blinked, feeling dazed, unable to decide which eye to focus upon. Each one was impenetrable and stationary, unlike its mouth that parted to proclaim neutrally:

"Ah… a table. One has become available. Very well. We are ready for you now. Come this way."

Madam Z parted the silk curtains with six of her eight limbs. The long white folds were tied off with spontaneous loops of thread, attaching them to the walls and ceiling. She then departed through the opening she had made.

Wyatt was happy to escape from this claustrophobic enclosure. He was surprised to find himself walking into an expansive meadow lush with plumes of greenery and cattails. The summer days of his youth came to mind. He saw Kat upon a slight rise, at the shoreline of a lake. She was seated at a table with Hazel, Harold and Izzy. As she waved at him, Wyatt noted she was handcuffed to a pole that went through the center of the table. It held aloft a red umbrella.

Wyatt noticed the other tables. All of them empty.

Wick was witnessing an entirely difference vista. He wasn't sure if he was hallucinating. He was shocked to see a little girl seated at a table chained to a pole. But instead of an umbrella, the pole had a tiny red flag – with the number 18 – flapping in the breeze. There were several more poles, none with tables attached, only flags. And each of these upright poles and flags was situated on a plateau of meticulously groomed lawn. And nearby, within this green rolling landscape were lakes of white sand abutting the greens.

"How very strange." Wick looked for his assistant to assist him. "This feels so familiar. And yet we have never seen this place before. Or have we? Here, Damian, carry my cane for me."

Damian took his cane and followed behind Wick.

"Wait up!" Riley appeared in the foyer.

Wick looked back to see Madam Z sealing the passageway into a solid curtain of white. He became distracted by white clouds in the sky. He wondered how this was possible. There were oak trees that receded into the horizon. The many haphazard lakes of sand were puzzling too. It was quite baffling. He had an urge to hit something. He retrieved his cane from his assistant. He stopped and turned it upside down, clutching the bottom of his cane with both hands. He imagined swinging the shaft and whacking a tiny ball with the club.

"*Strange*," Wick murmured aloud.

"What is?" asked Wyatt.

"This place!" said Wick. "I feel certain we've been here before. Perhaps the three of us. Ah, perfect, now we are a *foursome*."

"Don't be *daft*," squawked Riley, covering his hooded eyes with his goggles. "Look alive. Let's get on with this. Watch your steps. Follow close and be alert if you want to stay alive."

Riley knew this terrain was booby-trapped with land mines – triggered with pressure-sensitive spikes, or armed with trip wires. His unit was being decimated. He thought of the four he had lost. He wanted no more casualties. His infrared goggles were magnified to spot irregularities. And through the lenses the terrain had a dark green hue. It resembled a sickly twilight.

Wyatt and Wick could not comprehend why Riley kept hopping erratically off course, refusing to travel in a straight line. Despite this, they followed his lead and all four ascended the slope to reach the plateau where Kat and the others were seated.

Wick, speechless, stared at the little girl.

Riley yanked back his goggles to survey the table. "What the hell happened to Scarlet?"

"Missing in action," quipped Harold.

"She was struck!? Riley threw down his goggles.

"Calm down." Harold untied his bow tie and twirled it upon his fingers. "She went off to freshen up and change."

Riley spied the pitcher of yellow liquid set on the table. Kat was drinking from a glass. "I wouldn't drink that if I was you."

"But you aren't," said Kat with grin.

"I am not what?" Riley scowled.

"Me. It's only lemonade." Kat raised her eyebrows and sucked her straw. She stopped to ask the weasel, "Are you the Minister?"

Wick awakened from his paralysis of astonishment and touched his spectacles. "Good, Lordy! It *is* true. You must be the girl who fell from the sky."

"That would be me," said Kat.

Wick tapped his cane. "Minister—no. I am the *Prime* Minister. Elected in a landslide victory by the citizenry here."

She extended her chained arm as far as it would reach to shake his hand. "Pleased to meet you. What does a Prime Minister do?"

"He... I..." Wick paused to regard himself, his responsibilities, brushing imaginary dust off his shoulders and calling attention to his gold epaulettes. He finally noticed Kat's hand chained to a pole and extended toward him. "I preside. Lead and govern. I hope you can *appreciate* the challenge that comes from being the voice of so many. I must sacrifice my own mind for the masses. Becoming one for all and all for none... hum?" He was reluctant to touch the girl's pink flesh but forced himself to give her fingertips a quick shake. "Yes, well, welcome to Evolsdog."

"No!" squawked Riley, "She is *not* welcome. Not until we know *how* and *why* she came here!"

"Indeed, yes, why?" asked Wick. "And *how*... did you?"

"I wish I knew," said Kat.

"I suppose you now *wish* to stay?" asked Wick suspiciously.

"Thank you, no. I wish to leave. To go home."

"There. She *wishes* she knew and *wishes* to leave." Wick tapped his cane on the grass. "Well, that is a relief. I believe her."

Riley squawked, "No! She knows more than she's telling us."

"But that's not true," said Kat.

"I say you're a spy," said Riley. "Come on, wake up everyone! We're in the midst of a war here!"

"What war?" said Harold.

"On terror!"

"Where?" Wick looked around.

"Right under our *noses!*" Riley jerked his beak at Kat.

"Relax, Riley." Wyatt seated himself next to Hazel. He leaned back in his chair. "Try to enjoy this beautiful day."

"Beautiful?" Riley spat on the dirt. "Is everyone daft but me?" He looked down at the table where everyone was seated. He chose to remain standing. Izzy had dozed off again. He was critical of their lax behavior, drinking lemonade while their world was being compromised and undermined. "Anyone care to hazard a guess as to why all empires fall? *Anyone?*"

Except for the tranquil gurgle of liquid sucked through straws, Riley was met with a united non-participatory silence.

"Complacency!"

"Ah... it makes sense now." Wick took the glass of lemonade Damian had poured for him. "You're the chap I assigned to head our Department of Homeland Security. Riley, is it? Good show. Keep up the marvelous work."

Riley grumbled and sat. "To hell with it! I give up."

"Mustn't surrender too soon," Wick cautioned. "Very bad form. It gives the enemy the impression you are *losing*, don't you see? The art of diplomacy is having opinions with no conviction."

Riley rolled his eyes and poured himself a drink. Wick was now pontificating to no one in particular. Kat was watching Riley who stared back from across the table. "You claim to be an innocent *cat*, but once I apply the *screws* to you—" He pounded the table for effect, for all to hear. "You will be *singing* a different tune!"

Izzy snorted and woke. "Where was I?"

Wick overheard Riley and exclaimed, "Marvelous! What songs will she be singing?"

"I didn't know you sang, my dear," remarked Hazel.

"It's news to me," said Wyatt. "You sing?"

Kat didn't know how to answer. "I mean, I can. But not—"

"Fancy that," whistled Izzy, "a cat who sings!"

"Maybe she's a *bird*—not a cat!" Wick stood and turned his cane upside down, curiously experimenting. He applied practice strokes, brushing the wooden head of his cane upon the manufactured lawn. "Whatever made you think you were a cat?"

Kat sighed, "I never said I was."

"Wait until you hear Scarlet." Harold removed a tiny umbrella from a lemon slice floating in the pitcher of lemonade. He twirled it and told Kat, "She has a *lovely* singing voice."

"So does Hazel," said Wyatt, winking at the squirrel.

"I do *not*," laughed Hazel. She blushed, fanning her cheeks.

"Wait, I'm confused," said Izzy, directing his confusion at Riley. "*Screws,* you said? Are these screws used for tuning the girl?"

Riley ignored Izzy. He looked straight at Kat who looked back. The others were chattering madly among themselves about complete nonsense. Riley leaned forward to tell her in a hushed but forceful voice, "Don't forget what I said. Fear *is* your friend."

Kat asked him, "Why do you hate me?"

"I am here to *help* you."

"But you said you wanted to—"

Riley lurched—knocking over his chair. "What was that!? Get down everyone! Incoming!"

Kat was startled. The others were nonchalant, rather annoyed by Riley's disruptive behavior, gesturing for him to settle down.

The crow smoothed his feathered cape, still leery.

Kat was curious. "What did you hear, or see?"

"More than you want to know." Riley reseated himself.

Kat frowned. "Why did you lock me in a cage if you—"

"Listen to me! Do you think being outside your cage makes you more safe than being inside it?"

The cold glass of lemonade was sweating. It made her shiver and she removed her hand. "I don't know."

Riley smiled darkly. He pulled down his goggles. Against his black-feathered face, the green-tinted lenses gave him an eerie look. It made Kat shudder again.

The crow opened his beak. "Watch out for Scarlet."

chapter seven

Scarlet Fox

Scarlet Fox was peeking through a hole in the wall, watching the activity inside her Outside-In Palace. With a cunning smile, she went back to powdering her nose in the vanity mirror and mused about her next move. She admired herself. She loved the art of seduction. The theater. Where spectacles were created. A place of seeing. The application of black liner to her eyes was symbolic, a mask to hint at what she represented: twilight and feminine magic. She was known to be a trickster.

She liked what she saw in her mirror and through her portal. The palace was her stage, a blank slate on which to experiment with her customers, unbeknownst to them. She converted the decor to suit her moods and be adaptable to whatever theme she sought to present. For her new production she recruited the talents of Madam Z, whom she had heard of through innuendo and had investigated, searching the dark woods to see if the rumors about this arthropod were true. Satisfied she had met a kindred spirit, Scarlet hired Z to spin webbed backdrops throughout her palace. The ambience began in the foyer. Her guests would be mesmerized. The initiation was to prepare them for the vistas of sculpted interior to follow. The floor, ceiling and walls were fabricated out of tightly-woven iridescent silk. This undulating topography provided a canvas for her unsuspecting customers to project their subconscious minds upon. And for Scarlet to play with.

She called this new thematic adventure Dreamscapes.

Scarlet stood, smoothed the white silk dress woven by Madam Z to tightly conform to the contours of her body, then proceeded from the dressing room onto what appeared to be (viewed from the other side of the looking glass) a cumulus cloud onto which she alighted.

It was Harold who gasped. The others turned their heads too. They saw Scarlet emerging from the sky onto a puffy atmosphere, descending down a spiral staircase. Entranced by her entrance, they all sat in silence as she approached their table.

"Is everyone enjoying themselves?"

Harold's nose twitched. His facial fur had turned a pinkish hue. His foot thumped the lawn. And his naturally floppy ears began to stiffen. "Scarlet, y-you're... you—"

"Yes, Harry? What am I?"

"B-beautiful," he stuttered, "b-but I mean... I..."

Playing to the others too, she asked, "What *do* you mean?"

"I mean..." Harold glanced at Kat. "A little girl is present."

"We've met," said Scarlet. "Hello, again."

"Hello," said Kat.

"Is no one going to comment on my attire?" Scarlet moved her hips and lifted her arms into a statuesque pose.

"You look like a princess," said Kat.

"Why not a queen?" Scarlet playfully countered.

"Or that," said Kat with a smile. "You're very pretty."

"Why, thank you, little girl." Scarlet turned toward Wick whose mouth was open, at a loss for words. She feigned surprise, mocking him with an attitude of reverential contempt, "Well, if it isn't the Prime Minister himself. Have you come to grace my palace?"

Wick blushed. His whiskers twitched. Wanting to be chivalrous, he removed his top hat, but placed it upon his lap, too embarrassed to stand. He had become too aroused by her presence and opted to remain seated. He lifted his hand instead.

"What is this?" said Scarlet. "Am I to curtsy? Kiss your ring?"

"No, I–I..." stammered Wick. "I beg your pardon."

With a pout, Scarlet tapped her bejeweled finger upon the crown of his doffed hat. "Since you have come to *beg*. Granted. I forgive you. And pardon your misgivings."

Izzy was now fully awake. He was gawking at Scarlet's body, along with Riley and Wyatt.

Hazel lightly swatted her feather duster at Wyatt.

"What!? What was that for?"

"Don't tell me—*what?*" Hazel acted miffed and hurt.

"You can't expect me *not* to look," said Wyatt.

"Keep your eyes on me," said Hazel.

"It's not a crime to look," said Wyatt.

"For goodness sake, Scarlet." Hazel fanned her face and stood. "Put something on. You're indecent."

"Am I?" said Scarlet. "Do you find my outfit inappropriate?"

"I—It's…" sputtered Harold. "You're lovely."

"Why thank you, Harry." She touched his nose.

"A vision to *uphold*." Izzy was squinting to see her clearly.

"*Men,*" huffed Hazel, fluffing out her tail and walking away.

"Dessert?" announced Scarlet. "Who wants to eat cake?"

All the men quickly raised their hands in unison.

Kat raised her hand too.

Scarlet clapped her paws above her head, then sat upon the seat Hazel had vacated. "Are you enjoying yourself here, little girl? Are they treating you kindly?"

Kat raised her handcuffed wrist.

"Riley, you *bad* boy," Scarlet chastised. "Remove these cuffs this instant. I will not allow this punitive behavior in my establishment. Take them off—*immediately*. Or I will have to ask you to leave."

Kat was surprised that Riley obeyed her. He grumbled yet rose and came over, unlocking her wrists.

"Now say you are sorry," said Scarlet. "Not to me. To *her*."

Riley had difficulty removing his eyes from Scarlet.

"*Say* it," prodded Scarlet in a teasing manner.

Riley gave Kat a cynical grin. "I am regretfully… so *truly* sorry. Accept my apology for attempting to keep you *safe* and secure."

Kat was not comforted by his apology nor the sight of insects – six total, dressed in tuxedos, holding trays as they crawled up the slope toward them. With rapid precision they came, setting down an eclectic setting of forks, napkins, plates, cups and saucers. No two item matched in color or shape. Except for the pieces of grey cake resembling firewood burned to ash. Each chunk was adorned by a dollop of green sauce, trickling like slime down its sides.

Kat sat perfectly still, staring at her plate.

"Tea, coffee or cocoa?"

Kat looked up at the cricket. The ends of his antennae rubbed together twitching impatiently. He was waiting for her decision. He had three steaming pots in separate gloved hands.

"Cocoa, I guess," she said, then gasped, startled by the random splatters of hot liquid. The server had poured it rapidly into her tiny cup, and intentionally imprecise, she suspected, since no one else had received this sloppy service. The chirping waiters bustled around the table, then scampered away as quickly as they came.

"Time to eat," announced Scarlet. "Bon appétit!"

Kat watched the others as they cut with forks into the cake and speared pieces into their mouths, expressing delight, sipping their beverages, chattering among themselves as they ate. Scarlet observed Kat as she broke off a piece with her tarnished two-pronged fork and inserted it in her mouth – before spitting it back onto her plate.

"*Auugh*," said Kat, wiping her mouth and tongue with a napkin. "Sorry but... this tastes like... like..."

"Like what?" asked Scarlet.

"I don't want to be rude."

"Be rude. It is not my recipe. Say it," prodded Scarlet.

"I tastes like... ash. Topped with pond slime."

Scarlet laughed and clapped her bejeweled paws.

"You're not angry?" said Kat.

"Why would I be? You guessed correctly. Extraordinary. You are quite the curious one. What did you say you were again?"

Kat pushed away her plate. "A girl."

"Try the cocoa," said Scarlet.

Kat sniffed, wrinkling her nose. "Why? Is it mud?"

Delighted by her remark, Scarlet clapped. "Much worse. You are a clever girl. Far too clever to be here in our world."

"Your cake," said Harold, wiggling his nose, unable to take his eyes off her. "It's delicious, Scarlet."

"Why thank you, my Harry."

The others muttered their consent as they munched and drank.

Kat noticed how the others kept peering at Scarlet, which didn't seem unusual, at first, since she was the host and beautiful. But their eyes would either linger or take stealthy peeks before looking away. Which made Kat wonder.

"Why does everyone act so funny around you?"

"Funny in what way?"

"The way they keep looking at you."

"It's the price of fame." Scarlet batted her eyes.

"Are you famous?"

"To a few. Not to you." She narrowed her eyes with a sly smile. "It must be my beauty. Describe how they look at me."

"It's more... at your body."

Scarlet abruptly stood, which caused heads to turn. "What do you see, little girl?"

"A white dress," said Kat. "It's fun. I like the iridescence."

Scarlet sat back down, intrigued. "You *are* different."

"I'm a girl."

"More than that. You're extremely curious."

"Everyone's curious," said Kat.

"Not curious the way you are." Scarlet studied her. "Would you like to know my secret?"

Kat was suspicious but said, "Okay."

"Everyone here, except for you, thinks I am naked."

"But you're not."

"And..." Scarlet touched a red manicured fingernail to her lips.

"They believe they are eating chocolate cake topped with a cherry sauce and whipped cream."

"I don't understand," said Kat.

"Neither do they. It won't kill them. It's a harmless mind game. Pay no attention to them. They can't truly hear us at this moment. What do you think of my decor? The ambience I have designed?"

Kat looked around.

"Describe what you see."

"A large white room," said Kat. "Covered from floor to ceiling with silk. What do you see?"

"The same," said Scarlet. "But they do not. Which is why I find you so curious. Yes, a *curiosity* is what you are."

Kat was confused. "What am I supposed to be seeing?"

"When you entered the foyer you were meant to be *hypnotized*. Yet you failed to be."

"Sorry," said Kat.

"But if you *had*, you would be envisioning a world that is inside your head – projected upon my canvas. As the rest are. See?"

Wyatt was talking to Hazel, both turned in their seats, gazing at something the frog was pointing to on a blank wall. The crow was gesturing explosively with his wings and pointing at the surrounding floor to convince the beaver of something. The rabbit and weasel, with Damian at his side, had abandoned their seats. The rabbit had borrowed the frog's pine-needle walking stick and was holding it upside down. The weasel had reversed his cane. Both of them were intently stroking the clubs of their cane and stick against the ground, comparing techniques.

"What are they all doing?" asked Kat.

"You'd have to ask them," said Scarlet. "Honestly, I could care less as long as they have fun. That is my business."

"What is?"

"Providing entertainment. Converting the orthodox methods of fun into thinking outside of the box.”

“What box?”

Scarlet stood and extended her paw toward Kat.

“You will see. My box seats are deluxe. Come with me.”

“To where?” Kat hesitated, but took hold of Scarlet’s sleek paw which pulled Kat to her feet and kept hold of her hand.

“Believe me. You will not be missed.”

Kat glanced back at the table and recalled the crow’s warning. Riley was too preoccupied to notice her departure and she wondered now if she had been safer handcuffed to the table. “Where are you taking me?”

“There is no need to be afraid.”

“I’m not.”

“Nor should you *lie*.”

They ascended a white spiral staircase draped in a silky gauze. The iridescent mesh extended to the walls and ceiling, transforming corners into curves and made it difficult to discern where anything ended or began. Kat thought they were on the staircase Scarlet had used for her entrance. Then she noticed there were more spiraling staircases around the room, some going up, others down, to hidden passageways. At the top of the landing, two stories high, Kat looked back upon the others who were oblivious to their departure as the fox had predicted.

“This way,” instructed Scarlet, pulling Kat through an opening which led to another stairwell illuminated by translucent walls and steps that spiraled upwards. It wound around a circumference that continued to narrow and became transparent.

They arrived inside a glass cupola. It was situated at the top of the building. From this glass enclosure Kat had a panoramic view of the village, the tops of trees, the mountainside, and the rising mist through which she glimpsed a meadow far beyond. The place where she had awoken to discover a frog looking down at her. She also could see the path she had arrived on and the two rivers that merged into a waterfall at the bridge's entrance.

Looking down, Kat was alarmed to see the floor was made of glass. Beneath them was a crystal-clear view of the interior.

"Relax," said Scarlet. "Get comfortable."

There were only two chairs, each sculptured from blown glass. The arms, legs, back and seat were elegantly curved into the shape of flowers. A cluster of stamens and pistils formed the seat cushion. In between these seats was a glass table in the shape of a mushroom, which gave the appearance of having sprouted there naturally.

Kat timidly sat, expecting the glass to be hard and cold, but was surprised by its cushiony warmth. She gasped and let out a tiny yelp – aroused by the pleasurable sensation of heat entering her. It felt as if she had submerged her body into hot bath water, stimulating her skin with a rush of blood traveling straight to her head.

"*Oh,*" she said with a blush.

Scarlet settled her body into the other seat and sighed.

"Pleasurable, is it not?"

Kat nodded. "I can't believe I'm sitting on glass."

"You're not," said Scarlet. "You're simply imagining you are."

"But I'm seeing right through the chair. Through the floor too. It's very unsettling to feel like…"

"Nothing is there?"

"Yes," said Kat.

"Like we're suspended in air?"

"Yes."

"Now you know how it feels. To be me."

Kat didn't know what to think. She was so overwhelmed by the warmth massaging her and pulsating through her body.

"Can you imagine living with this constant awareness every day, knowing that so many – the *multitude* – are thinking about *me*."

"Are they?"

"Not every second. But several times a day. That, dear creature, is the cost of fame. Having the power to attract and influence the behavior of others. Do you *know* how that makes me feel?"

Kat shook her head.

"Empowered." Her lips had the hint of a smile as Scarlet closed her dark eyes. "It is *intoxicating*."

Wanting to impress this fox, Kat blurted, "Intoxication. I know what that means. To feel stimulation, excitement, stupefaction."

Scarlet half opened her eyes with a frown. "You know words. If you *knew*, you would know it is a sensation far greater than that."

Kat wasn't sure what to think. She felt herself floating upon a warm bed of air, a transparent cloud, looking over the arms of her chair and between her legs. There were several rooms beneath them. She not only saw the frog, squirrel, crow, beaver, rabbit, weasel and groundhog moving in one room, but she saw more animals moving about in other rooms. It reminded her of a beehive.

"What are they all doing down there?" asked Kat.

Scarlet opened her eyes to give Kat her full attention. "Think not of them. It is only you and me now. The rest of the world has faded from view. Into another level. You feel this, yes?"

Kat nodded. "I guess. I do feel different, somehow."

"More aware? More alive?"

Kat looked around at all the glass supporting her, how she could peer through everything and how it seemed she was suspended in air. "It feels unreal. Strange. To be so high and able to see all around, in every direction. Both inside and outside."

"An elaborate illusion created by the use of mirrors."

"Are you serious?"

Scarlet narrowed her lined eyes with the hint of a blasé smile. "Don't be naive. Look at me. What do you see?"

The space between them appeared to close. Kat was drawn into this animal's mysterious black eyes. "A fox."

"You hesitated. The image of what you *think* you see of me is of no real concern to me."

This unsettled Kat. "I thought that's what you were. Sorry."

"Sorry for what? I *am* a fox. You are trying too hard to please. Do not. It is unbecoming and unflattering. Why do you *care* what others think of you?"

"Shouldn't I?"

"No. Care about yourself. Care what *you* think about yourself. Care to know what is inside *your* mind, before others decide."

"But that's being selfish. And self-centered?"

"Who *else* can you be, if not you? So be yourself. Before others implant their idea of what they think you should be. This is how you become yourself. Which is someone you have *yet* to be."

"I know who I am," said Kat.

"Do you?"

"Yes. I'm a girl whose name is Kathlyn. Also Kat."

"And what is that?"

"Someone who has *feelings*," said Kat.

"Whose feelings are hurt." Scarlet added, "But have now been exposed to desire and pleasure. You will admit that, yes?"

Kat nodded, squirming in her seat. She wasn't sure if she should be feeling as much pleasure as she was. "I don't know what you're doing. Or what you want from me."

"For you to avoid stagnating. To grow like a delicious grape."

"Why?" said Kat.

Scarlet reached over to touch Kat's hand. "In order to ripen."

Kat pulled her hand away. "Meaning what?"

Scarlet gave a teasing laugh and reached into the air to mime the plucking of fruit off a vine. She placed the imaginary grape between her lips to crush and suck its juices. "To ferment and mature like a fine wine."

"Please," said Kat, "can we go back now?"

"We can never go back. There is only going forward."

Kat moved to get off the seat. "Forward then."

"Stay put!" scolded Scarlet.

"Why?"

"I am not done with you yet," she joked. "I have decided to help you. I am offering you a place to stay. To become my protégé."

"Why?"

"You will learn to entertain. I will teach you the art of pleasure, more of this. I insist, there is no better life. Together we will have the entire village coming to us. Star attractions."

"That's... very generous, but—"

"Yes?"

"I would very much like to go home. For now."

Scarlet drummed her fingernails lightly, yet displayed only mild disappointment. She exhaled a dismissive laugh. "Only *once* does an opportunity come like this. Twice would be nice. But do not count on it happening. Promise me one thing before I let you go."

"What?"

"Will you promise me?"

"That depends. On what it is you want me to promise."

"A good question." Scarlet gave her a nod. "*Know* your passion. You will never be fully alive without passion. Feel it course through your veins, your blood, this passion. Do you feel it?"

Kat felt the pulsating warmth from the glass stamen and pistils and she blushed, uncertain what this pleasure meant.

"I do."

Scarlet smiled. "Then you are ready. To change your mind and remain with me. A haven awaits of endless frolic and ecstacy."

"Thank you, but..." said Kat, "I would like to go home."

"What is home? *This* is home. Everyone will flock to see you. This curiosity. This shining star. I will guide you."

"Again, thank you..." Kat was intimidated by the eyes of this fox which never strayed from hers. "May I go now?"

"If that is your wish." Scarlet moved her elegant paw along the armrest. Lights glowed off and on at the touch of her fingers.

"What are you doing?" asked Kat.

"Choosing where to send you. You *too* see reality differently, yet not the same as me. Mirrors are funny things. Did you know that many creatures don't recognize their reflection as being themselves. A cat may cringe or howl. I am simply explaining how differently others may perceive you. One world. Multiple visions."

"I'll remember that. Thank you. May we go?"

"Others care what I say and do. But do I care? Not at all. Ah, but do you care?"

Kat smiled a fraction. "Not really."

Scarlet smirked and laughed. "That *is* the answer."

The fox pressed the armrest activating a glowing red light.

"Be sure to keep me in your heart. Remember. Fun requires an element of shock. So take this. A forget-me-not."

Scarlet waved her painted fingernails.

Kat screamed as her seat dropped out from under her, plunging her down a ramp, an incline, a slide – shooting her around and around until she shot through a paper-thin wall, becoming airborne. She kicked and flailed, but to no avail, like a bird freefalling from its nest. Expected to fly. But crash-landing and splattering into a pile of discarded fruit.

She had landed in a dumpster.

In shock, Kat examined the mess she sat in – the sticky husks of pomegranates and baskets of mashed strawberries having spoiled. The more she tried to excavate herself the more she sullied herself. Red juices were streaked and running down her arms and legs. Her white sockings, red dress, and underwear were stained.

After luxuriating in such pleasure, such warmth – as if being on top of the world, then sinking so low, feeling so cold, and unclean –

to be discarded like garbage, felt horrible.

Kat began to cry.

chapter eight

Camille Chameleon

Camille Chameleon was riding on a wave, clinging to the wood railing of a three-masted schooner. Or so she imagined, swaying on a branch interacting with a gentle breeze, but feeling on vacation, her eyelids sealed shut, envisioning her island destination of Crete coming into view. When suddenly she heard a splash. Someone had plunged overboard. Her eyes opened. Half of her vision rotated to the west, while the other half rotated toward the east. Both eyeballs then synchronized and looked south, quick to focus on a floating patch of oceanic debris. Some thing or someone was writhing in the muck, about to drown.

More curious than compassionate, Camille ventured out upon the tree limb to investigate. She moved methodically, her claw-like hands and legs mechanically clutching the branch to position herself for a better look. When she realized it was the little girl she had almost snagged earlier, but had gotten away, Camille licked her lips. This, she knew, would require a combination of skill and luck to attach and reel-in a creature of this magnitude. But she was willing to try. Her two independent eyes rotated to calculate the depth and stereoscopic location, prior to launching forth her elastic tongue to club her victim with a suction cup.

Kat was wiping at tears, smearing pomegranate and strawberry juices with the back of her hands, making a bigger mess of herself, when struck by a wad of something.

"Aauh!" she screamed, desperately fighting to remove the glob of muscle and mucus attached to her torso and legs. She was yanked up a fraction, before dropping back into the garbage bin. She kept being shaken about and glanced up to see her attacker. Angered, she reached up and grabbed the sinewy tongue and yanked hard.

Camille, caught off guard by this counter attack, lost her grip, slipped and clipped her chin on the branch before springing down to the dumpster to land on top of Kat.

"Get off me!" shouted Kat, knocking Camille aside and peeling off the sticky glob attached to her.

Sucking in her tongue, Camille gulped and smiled.

"What is *wrong* with you? Stop doing that!"

Kat scooted to get further away from this horny creature whose eyeballs kept twirling about independently.

"Sorry." Camille settled her eyes into a synchronized blink.

"Why do you keep doing that?"

"Habit. It's... well, I wanted to get to know you."

"You were trying to *eat* me," accused Kat.

"Oh, please," said Camille, straightening her mussed garment, "you taste like spoiled strawberries and pomegranates. I don't know why I even bothered."

"Do you annoy everyone this way?"

"Can't we be friends?"

Camille extended her pincher-like hand with its fused fingers and thumb. Hesitating to touch it, Kat watched its skin tone transform from red to orange before she did, briefly, as a peace offering.

"Why do you want to be my friend?"

"I have so few," said Camille.

"Why am I not surprised?" Kat tried to stand, but fell back into the slippery unsteady muck.

"Allow me." Camille got to her feet, bolstered by her prehensile tail attached to the dumpster. She extended her hand once again.

Kat took hold this time and was helped to the front of the trash bin where she gripped its metal edge. Startled next by Camille's tail circling her body and hoisting her up and over then placing her down upon the ground. Camille hopped beside her.

"Why were you playing in the garbage?"

"I wasn't *playing*," said Kat.

"Oh?"

"No. Someone dumped me there."

"And that *someone*... would it be Scarlet Fox?"

"You know her?"

"As well as one can. Scarlet is so full of herself," said Camille. "She is both a curse and a blessing. I am glad she disposed of you."

"Why?"

"Now *we* can be friends." Camille furled her tail into a tight coil and strutted down the dappled alleyway. "But first we need to get you cleaned up. Come with me."

Kat felt she had no choice but to follow. She was now a mess. Her dress was soiled, smelling of fruit, and clammy against her skin.

"Where are we going?"

"To my habitat." Camille rotated her head and eyes backwards. "I *had* been on vacation before you plunged into that dumpster and took me off course."

"Sorry," said Kat, catching up to the chameleon who had veered from the alley onto a flagstone path. It wove through the backyards and backwoods of homes and shops. An archipelago of stepping stones on which she kept hopping from one to the next. "Can you please slow down?"

Camille abruptly stopped. "Am I going too fast? I get carried away. I forget my own mind sometimes. Where was I?"

"Taking me to your home, I think."

"Was I? I was. Over there. Across that log."

They now stood before a creek. Spanning the water from shore to shore was a fallen tree shorn clean of both its bark and branches. Kat looked but saw no structure on the other side.

"Wrong angle." Camille giggled. "Look up."

Through a mishmash of pussywillows and tall grass Kat spotted stairs winding around a redwood tree. "You live in a tree house?"

"With a most exciting view."

The composite of stacked cubicles midway up the tree were very colorful but appeared to have been constructed haphazardly, which sharply contrasted the meticulously built – though equally bizarre – structures she had seen throughout the village. These walls were far from plumb, but askew, balanced precariously upon the branches.

"Is it safe?" ask Kat.

Camille laughed and echoed, "Is it safe? Is anything?"

The chameleon hopped upon the log and moved along with ease, swishing her furled tail for balance. Kat stepped onto the tree trunk and was reassured by its circumference – twice as wide as she was – and its sturdiness. Kat, agile by nature, had perfect balance and gave passing glances at the water moving beneath her. But she was forced to stop when the chameleon stopped midway across the log.

Camille turned to say, "You need a change of clothing."

"I'll be fine," said Kat, maintaining her balance.

"Nonsense. I have oodles of things for you to wear."

"I'm almost dry. I can wash up when—"

"Suit yourself." Camille pivoted around and knocked Kat off the log with her long tail. "Oopsy-daisy!"

Kat plunged underwater to resurface screaming. "You did that on purpose!"

"Now look at you – *all* wet. Let me get you out of there."

Camille unfurled her tail to quickly dip it in the water to scoop up Kat before she was swept downstream. Camille then scampered across the remaining length of the log, pulling Kat in the water and creating a wake – before beaching her on the opposite shore of sand. Camille hopped off the log into the grass. With her tail still wrapped around Kat, she hoisted Kat up and down – to be dipped in water, shook in the air, then deposited dripping wet upon the grass.

"There," said Camille. "You've been cleansed. Brand new."

"I'm *soaked*," said Kat. "Thanks to you."

"Let's get you up that tree to dry."

The rickety stairwell that wound its way around the tree felt like something Kat might have built if she had the slightest knowledge of carpentry. The landing platform, serving as the porch, consisted of several planks of wood nailed to the uneven extension of branches. Kat clutched what she could to steady herself and followed Camille through two doors that swung open in the middle. They reminded her of saloon doors she'd seen in movies. Westerns. But that's where the cowboy theme ended. The interior walls had been whitewashed then blasted with spattering bursts of color which competed with the wild assortment of furniture. There was a chair with claws for feet. An ottoman shaped like a toadstool. A floor lamp designed with writhing snakes, three intertwined boas, emerging to form the shaft, rising into a symmetry of open jaws that held a globe.

Passing through several cubicles and doorways, Camille paused within an open space, presumably the living room. Open doors led out to an uneven deck directly over the river far below.

"Shall I brew us some tea?" said Camille. "We could sit on the deck and contemplate our navels on this glorious day."

"I'm cold," said Kat. "Also wet."

"Then let's hang you out to dry," laughed Camille.

"I'm also dripping water on your floor."

"I designed my place to accommodate leaks. Water falls through the cracks."

"How clever." Kat's tone had a tinge of sarcasm.

"Don't be *rude*." Camille's body changed from yellow to green to magenta in a flash, before settling back to become aqua blue.

"Are you all right?"

"I've never been better. Come."

Kat followed her into another room strewn with piles of colorful clothing across the floor and garments hanging from poles.

"This will be fun. Give me your dress."

"No. Why?"

"It's wet. Your socks and shoes too. Don't be shy."

"What am I supposed to wear?"

Camille picked up a towel off the floor and tossed it at her.

Kat sniffed the towel. "I'm not going to wear *this*."

Camille glowered, sucking in air to gradually recompose herself. After a few seconds she returned from an annoyed orange to a placid blue. "The towel is to wear before you decide *what* to wear."

Kat scrunched her brow, but disappeared behind a partition of hanging sheets. She kicked out her shoes, threw over her stockings, then flung her red dress over the top.

"What about the rest?" said Camille.

"The rest of what?"

"Everything. Don't you trust me?"

"Should I?"

"Your *things* will be hung out to dry in the sun."

"Fine." Kat tossed over her underpants too. She then emerged from behind the curtain wrapped in the towel.

"You behave as if I'm asking you to forfeit your skin. I never suspected you of being a snake. Are you?"

"Of course not." Kat knotted the towel tighter.

"Good." Camille gathered up the garments, pinching them between thumb and fingers. "Snakes are not my favorite creatures. Now stay put."

The chameleon exited to weave her way back to the living room where she stepped onto the deck. She flung Kat's clothing onto a few branches exposed to sunlight.

Kat was busy meandering through the assortment of clothing.

Camille returned to ask, "Find anything you like?"

"I'll just wait for my things to dry."

"Don't be silly. Let us play dress up." Carmen removed her soiled dress, tossing it aside, and stepped into a gauzy purple gown. Try something on while I try on these boots. How about these?"

Kat looked at the offerings. One was a beaded green dress and the other looked to be a leather jacket with purple tassels.

"That's not me."

"What *is* you?"

"I don't know. But I wouldn't be caught dead wearing *those*."

"You might be surprised. See if they fit you."

Kat watched as Camille kicked off the sneakers she had been wearing and pulled on a boot. It was brown suede with laces that came up to her knee. On her other foot she put on a hiking boot make of black leather which came up only to her ankle. She stood, admiring them both, then looked up at Kat.

"What do you think?"

"About what? The boots? They don't match."

"I know!" laughed Camille. "It is the latest fashion craze."

"Since when?"

"Since now. The two of us will start a trend."

"I don't think so."

"You are such the little pessimist."

"I am not," said Kat. "I'm being realistic. Don't you have pants I could wear? Or a simple skirt?"

"Nothing I have here is simple. I don't believe in simple."

"Blue jeans?"

Camille's spiky skin began to turn violet.

"*Fine*." Kat took what Camille had given her and went behind the partition. "I'll try them on. But this dress... I mean, it looks more like something a... you know, a..."

"A what?

"A girl wouldn't wear."

"You are no longer a girl."

"What is that supposed to mean? I am too."

"You're a young woman. In need of branching out. Blossoming. You cannot be little forever. Let me have a look."

Kat came out from behind the sheets wearing the beaded dress. She held up the top with her hands. "I feel ridiculous."

Camille came toward her, twirled her around and zipped up the back. "There. It fits you like a glove."

She spun Kat around and frowned. Kat was still holding up the top of the dress.

"Except for... well. You will continue to blossom. Now go and put on the jacket. Button it to the top."

Kat was pushed toward the partition, but looked back. "Don't you have something more..."

Camille's eyes rotated, aiming at her like guns on a turret.

"Right, I got it," Kat groused, disappearing behind the curtain. "Beggars can't be choosers? Do you at least have a mirror so I—"

"There are no mirrors here."

"*That* I can believe," muttered Kat while putting on the jacket. The chameleon's statement piqued her curiosity. "Why?"

"Personally, these portals don't frighten *me*."

"Portals?

"Ruled to be contraband by our ex-judge. Prior to going mad, himself. Or so the rumors fly."

"Mirrors are illegal? Why?" said Kat. "What rumors?"

"A few too many souls got lost and never found. Mirrors can't reflect who we truly are. Simply by looking. Do you want to hear what I say?"

Kat, buttoning the leather jacket, wasn't sure she did. "What?"

"It's a conspiracy," said Camille. "To keep us imagining we are something we are not." She brushed back the veil to a purple hat she placed on her head. "I don't need any mirror telling me who I am. I know myself. Others can imagine what they like."

Kat was puzzled by the chameleon's words as she emerged from behind the curtain. She peered critically at the jacket's purple fringe. Her hands held down the hem of the green-beaded miniskirt.

Camille sucked in her breath. "I am *green* with envy. Literally. Look at me. Look at you!"

"I look like a hooker."

Camille was fluffing her own dress. "What's a hooker?"

"Don't you think the dress is… like, a tad skimpy, a bit short?"

"Are you cold?"

"Maybe a pair of tights. Got any?"

Camille rummaged through the pile of garments, tossing up one thing after another in the air, until she exclaimed, "Eureka!"

"What?"

"The perfect mismatch." Camille displayed her discovery. Black and white harlequin tights. "And—I found you footwear!"

Snatching both items from the chameleon's pinched fingers, Kat stared with disbelief at the jester pants. With a sigh, she struggled to squeeze them on. Surprisingly they fit. The red ballet slippers too. Kat took a moment to laugh at herself.

"I look like the illegitimate child of Peter Pan and Tinkerbell."

"Who?"

"Never mind. They were make-believe. He was this boy who never grew up. And she was this tiny flittering fairy."

Camille was overjoyed. "I chose well then! Off we go!"

Startled – pulled by the hand – Kat followed this chameleon back through the warren of inner spaces. They paused in the living room as Camille peered outside, puzzled by something.

"What are you looking at?" Kat then saw her panties hanging off a branch and about to fall.

"Hey, are those my—"

Camille pulled Kat by the tassels of her jacket. "Come."

They wound their way down the tree stairs and were navigating through the tall grass and reeds when Kat saw an alligator lounging on the shore. She stopped. The animal was sprawled in the mud. And wearing a red dress.

"Hey! Wait. Is that? That's mine!"

"Good luck in getting it back." Camille hopped upon the log.

"Are you coming or going?"

Kat saw Camille crossing the creek and she raced to catch up, following the chameleon as she dashed through a maze of backyards and alleyways, eventually losing sight of her. Kat was out of breath as she emerged onto a cobblestone street. It was lined on both sides with curving sidewalks, boxed trees and flowers, and a variety of quaint storefronts. She felt conspicuous and ridiculous, out of place, especially dressed as she was, among this bustling crowd of creatures who paused to gawk at her. She was relieved to find Camille seated at an outdoor cafe. She was easy to spot because of the purple haze of a dress she was wearing, along with her two mismatched boots. While waving at Kat with one arm, she fluffed at the fabric of her gown with the other.

"I saved you a place," said Camille. "Come sit with me."

Kat sat beside her and tried to ignore all the attention they were receiving.

"See how wonderful it is being different?"

"Everyone is staring at us," said Kat.

"It is better to be noticed than ignored. Be different."

"Not if you're being teased and laughed at," said Kat.

"They are jealous." Camille opened her menu.

Kat picked up her menu but kept watch of a gang of children – rats, in fact – roughly jostling and playing amongst themselves in the street. They were glancing at Kat and laughing. One appeared to be the ringleader, or instigator. He was tossing pebbles at the other rats. Kat feared he was preparing to throw something at her next.

Camille glanced up, noticing this little bully about to toss a rock. She shot her tongue at him – striking him in the cheek and dragging him across the cobblestones. She brought him close to her face, then spat him out onto the sidewalk.

"Hey! You can't do that!" said the rat, swiping his face.

"Really? I just did. How does it feel being picked on?"

The boy got up, wiping the slime off his clothes. Backing away with his wounded pride, he said, "Weirdos! Leave me alone!"

"You will be – all *alone* – if you keep acting like a *brat*."

Camille turned and winked at Kat.

Kat smiled and confessed, "I'm beginning to like you."

"Beginning? I liked you from the moment you arrived."

"You did not," said Kat.

"Did too. I found you interesting. Different. I ordered us a plate of chocolates."

"I like chocolates."

"And sherbert wine."

"I don't drink wine," said Kat.

"Don't be silly," said Camille. "Everyone drinks wine."

A penguin waddled over to their table holding a large tray. Kat was distracted by his bow tie and tuxedo. It appeared to blend into his fur. He had flat protruding shoes and a long narrow nose with spectacles pinched near his eyes, black and beady, which gave him a serious demeanor. Without speaking a word he set down the dessert platter. From a carafe containing a slushy liquid he poured and filled two wine glasses, bowed, and departed.

"Perfecto!" Camille clapped her approval. She picked up her wine glass. "We must celebrate. I propose a toast."

"To what?"

"To anything. That racoon across the street rooting through the garbage. Look how neat and thorough he conducts himself sorting for recyclables. With such dignity. Admirable. Or how about that peacock coming toward us. Notice, she holds not one of her many purchases, instead has her two lap dogs carrying the packages for her. And look. She takes the lead, keeping them both on leashes. What a strange world. Let us toast to that."

Kat raised her glass. "The world *is* rather strange."

Camille clinked Kat's glass with hers. "I know. I just said that.

And to *us*. A toast to us!"

Kat watched the chameleon slurp the frothy liquid. Kat winced as she took a taste of the bittersweet cocktail.

Camille was pouring more for herself. "Icy. Be careful. If you drink it too fast. Head rush!"

To be polite Kat took a larger sip. "It's... different."

Camille gave a laugh. "Being homogeneous has its place. If you are *milk*. Being different is an acquired taste. Have a chocolate."

Each was a little dollop ranging in shades of darkness and sat in crinkly pastel doilies. Camille unwrapped a chocolate candy and plopped it in her mouth.

Kat removed one and took a tentative bite. "Wow. These are really good."

"Of course they are. Yet *bitter* without all the sugar and spice. Have as many as you like. No judgement here. As you see, I am, admittedly, a *gourmand*."

"That means you're a lover of food," said Kat, showing off her knowledge of words.

"And a glutton too." Camille hiccuped.

While munching on a chocolate and sipping her slushy drink, Kat looked around and realized how strange it was – to have fallen into a world where animals behaved like humans. That, in itself, was strange enough. But to now have it feel perfectly normal was all the more stranger. It seemed somehow natural that she was seated next to a colorfully eccentric chameleon who used her nasty tongue to lash out at others, and that she would be receiving the passing glances of a blue-faced baboon, or a toothy leopard, or some spikey big-nosed porcupine.

"Curiouser and curiouser," Kat mused, before it occurred to her she had spoken aloud, allowing her thoughts to slip out.

"What was that you said?" asked Camille

Kat shook her head, a bit confused. She decided she would take another swallow. She was now enjoying the taste, and ate another chocolate. She had lost count. Each one was so sweet and different. The day had taken on a lightness, a levity felt from the gentle breeze as she watched leaves tumbling along the cobblestones. It was easy to imagine being lifted in a gust of wind to float out of her chair and tumble head over heels down the street.

Camille said, "I *dare* you. To do something."

Kat looked at the chameleon whose face was a cloudy vision of sparkling iridescence.

"Do what?"

"Something outrageous."

"What, exactly?"

"Stand up and yodel? Twirl your arms. Do a pirouette!"

"Why would I do that?

"To declare your independence."

Kat frowned as she sipped her drink. "From what?"

"From what everyone is expecting of you. To be conventional. To blend in. To march in step. Follow the leader. Live a *bourgeois* life. Look how unhappy everyone is."

Kat looked around. "They seem pretty happy."

"Look closer," said Camille, smoothing her scarf.

"They're also looking at us. At *me*."

"Because they desire to be us."

"I don't think that's why they're looking," said Kat.

"I can make them stop looking."

"How?"

"Do you trust me?"

"Not really," said Kat.

Camille laughed. With a snap of her tongue she plucked the chocolate out of Kat's hand.

"Hey!"

"I don't really trust you either."

"That wasn't very nice."

"But a nice trick. What tricks do you know?"

"I don't know any tricks."

"Sure you do," said Camille. "You can sit up? Roll over?"

Kat furrowed her brow, then replied with playful sarcasm, "Sure. I can play dead too."

"Too easy. Can you stand on your head?"

"If I had to," said Kat. "Except I don't."

"Wanna make a bet?"

Kat became suspicious. "What kind of bet? What would I win?"

"Whatever it is you most desire."

"To go home," said Kat.

"Doable." Camille slapped her palms. "I can show you how."

"You can?"

"Only if you win. If I win, you have to stand on your head."

"Why?"

"To play the fool. Do you accept the bet, and the rules?"

Kat took a thoughtful sip. "What's the catch?"

Camille selected a chocolate and tossed it overhead, catching it in her mouth and swallowing. "I will *catch* any chocolate you throw into the air. It doesn't matter how high. If I fail to catch it, you win. But if I catch it, which I will, you lose. How does that sound?"

"Not very difficult. For you." Kat was nevertheless intrigued by the challenge, was feeling mischievous and wanted to go home. She began calculating how she could outsmart this chameleon. "I'll do it if we make it two. I'll bet that you can't catch *two* chocolates."

"At once!?" Camille rolled her eyes to dramatically express how difficult that would be, how it handicapped her odds of succeeding. "I would like to keep you. Around. As a friend. Plus, I hate to lose. But I will agree to your offer."

"To get me home if I win? You promise?"

"Absolutely."

"How can I know you're telling me the truth?"

"You cannot. No one can." Camille waved over passersby who had slowed to gawk at Kat. "If you want to watch a couple of freaks perform their magic, stay put." She sipped her drink and brushed the fringe on Kat's leather jacket. "I have been many things, but I am not a liar. To prove I am not, I will give you a clue."

"What kind of clue?"

"The kind that unlocks the door that will grant you your wish. The key is hanging around your neck."

Kat looked down and touched the necklace. "This?"

"No. What's inside."

"It opens?"

"I said a *clue*," said Camille peevishly. "Not the answer. Now, are you going to toss the chocolates in the air and play, or not?"

Kat stood and took two of the chocolates off the plate. A crowd had formed and was distracting her concentration.

"Focus on me," said Camille. "On winning."

Kat held one in each hand, moving them both up and down as if preparing to launch them vertically but – to everyone's surprise – flung them horizontally in opposite directions.

Having been so confident of her victory, Kat was baffled by her loss, being outsmarted, to be standing on her head on the sidewalk. She remembered her lesson in gym class, to first crouch and position her knees upon her elbows, before extending her legs slowly into the air where they wavered, balanced precariously, wigging her feet.

"Bravo!" Camille clapped her hands and encouraged the crowd to join in, which they did. "I knew you had it in you!"

Upside down, but coming into focus, Kat saw a puzzling sight. Coming toward her down the street were faces she recognized. They resembled a frog, crow, squirrel, rabbit, beaver, fox, weasel and groundhog. As they got closer and closer she was quite sure it was not her imagination. Wyatt, Riley, Hazel, Harold, Izzy, Scarlet, Wick and Damian were veering toward the cafe.

Scarlet said, "Look who has become a circus animal."

Riley squawked. "*How* did you escape us? And *why!?*"

Kat dropped back to her knees, feeling dizzy as she stood.

"Please, go away," said Camille, pulling down her veil. "The two of us were having a little romp, a tete-a-tete, enjoying ourselves."

"Ya is one slippery *cat*," Izzy said. "Like an eel, ain't cha?"

"I am not an eel," said Kat, "and I didn't—"

"Didn't what?" asked Harold, holding his pen and notepad.

"Try to escape! *She*—tossed me out. Into the trash!"

Scarlet ignored the accusation. "What a wild imagination this itty-bitty girl has. Tell them where I took you."

Kat rubbed her eyes, shielding them from the sun. "Up winding stairs to a room made entirely of glass. The chairs too. I could see through everything, outside *and* inside. Right through the floor to the room below. Where I could see all of you. And that's—"

"Marvelous!" exclaimed Wick, tapping his cane. "If only I could trick my constituents so brilliantly as Ms. Fox. Marvelous."

"But you do, Sir," said his assistant.

"Thank you, Damian. Now be quiet," he hissed, then his voice boomed to be heard by the masses who had gathered. He turned back to Scarlet. "Kudos, mademoiselle. What a trickster you are. What an outstanding performance!"

"What are you *talking* about?" said Kat.

"She hypnotized us all," Wyatt told her.

"That was part of the entertainment," said Hazel. "I could have sworn I was on a tropical beach."

"Just the two of us," added Wyatt with a smile.

Harold was scratching his ears. "Extremely puzzling really. She had me knocking around this tiny white ball."

"I did nothing at all," said Scarlet. "It was all *your* doing."

"Nevertheless," continued Harold, "though it was a lovely day,

I found myself on a groomed patch of grass trying desperately to get that little ball to drop in a hole. Wick was there too!"

"It's true," said Wick. "And where were you?"

"Don't even ask," grumbled Riley.

"In some dam hazardous terrain," said Izzy. "So he claimed. Ya stupid fool, you had me convinced of it too."

"Deja *vu*," said Riley. "I knew that battlefield. I'd been there. And don't tell me otherwise!"

"So long as everyone had fun," said Scarlet.

"I can't say I did," groused Riley.

"It was a harmless diversion," said Scarlet. "You went where your mind wanted you to go. You were players in my theater."

"Not me," said Kat, "and it *wasn't* my imagination."

The others turned to regard her.

Kat pointed. "She... this... *fox*, dropped me down a slide where I ended up in a pile of garbage!"

Camille sipped her wine. "I can vouch for that. I found her in the trash. She was filthy. I had her cleaned and spruced her up."

Scarlet was quick to laugh. "The trash? Now *who* is going to believe another one of your conspiracy theories, Camille?

"Nice outfit," said Wyatt, smiling as he tipped his beret at Kat.

Kat flushed. "I didn't have a big choice in the selection."

Hazel gave her jacket a light dusting.

"She's being modest," said Camille. "I love her taste. Her attire is very liberating."

"Yes, *liberal*," said Wick. "As opposed to being conservative. However, I swing both ways."

"He aims for the middle ground," stated Damian.

"I do," said Wick, "I take all sides, representing both the left *and* the right. That is not to say I cannot be swayed, yet I hold firmly to my core convictions. Can I count on your vote next election?"

"She doesn't *live* here, Wick," snarled Riley.

"Well, yes, no. But once she applies for citizenship."

"She's a loose gear," said Izzy, "and ain't fit to be here."

"Not true," said Camille. "She has begun to blend in nicely."

Scarlet was smug. "Coming from you that is quite a testament. How has life been treating you, Camille?"

"Like a cabaret, Scarlet. One never knows what role one will be cast into next."

"Touché," said Wyatt.

Prior to standing on her head, then righting herself on two feet, Kat had been feeling relaxed, close to normal, lighter than air. But now her head had begun to spin and sputter like a punctured balloon leaking helium. She was mildly alarmed when she saw the platter of remaining chocolates coming toward her, getting larger, before her vision went blank and her head crashed into the table.

"Incoming!" shouted Riley, flipping down his goggles. "The girl has been hit! Look out!"

"*No*," said Scarlet calmly, "she has lost consciousness."

"Again?" said Wyatt. "This is the same way I found her."

"You told us she fell from the sky," said Harold.

"You lied!?" said Riley. "You didn't find her in a meadow?"

"Unconscious," said Wyatt, "that is what I meant."

Hazel aimed her duster at Camille. "What nonsense have you been feeding this little girl and filling her head with?"

"Oh, please," said Camille.

The others watched her flip back her purple veil and gulp down the last of her wine before she addressed them all, separately, eyes rotating independently in their protruding sockets.

"The little girl needs to know she's a freak. I was helping her to *embrace* that fact. To celebrate her arrival and departure from the norm. Has anyone looked at themselves lately? Am I the only one who is not *delusional* and can recall who we were before we got here in the first place!?"

Her question was met by silence. Her face and entire body had turned a violent red.

"It's why mirrors can't be trusted. They give false impressions. They capture our imagination and prevent self-reflection — the only way to know who we truly are."

Camille stood and snagged the last of the fallen chocolates off the sidewalk with her quick tongue. Licking her lips, she strutted off with her tail recoiled, disappearing down an alleyway.

chapter nine

Owen Owl

Owen Owl was a doctor, a general practitioner, who was alarmed by his own urges – wanting to eat his patients. He could not comprehend what inner demons caused this impulse, these errant thoughts to combine forces again. He thought he had driven them away, broken them asunder, to be gone from his mind forever. But they had stormed back. The alarm expressed on his patient's face was indisputable. A little wide-eyed mouse with his furry cheeks and pink lips quivering. His four siblings intimidated too. They were clearly cognizant (though too immature to articulate what they knew to be true) what they sensed hidden behind his eyes. Even his jovial chuckle as he blinked behind his monocle, which he removed, intending to reassure them with a smile, to let them know their fears were groundless, had proven ineffective. The runt of the litter began to whimper.

"Stop sobbing," scolded his mother, who was there to hug and wipe his eyes, reassuring her children. Though intimidated herself, she smiled bravely. "The good doctor only wants to help us."

The women's courage was admirable, thought Owen. She was delicious to look at, mildly plump, making her even more appealing. He discretely wiped his mouth which curved downward to form the semblance of a blunt beak. Together with his large eyes, he had the features of a night owl, or so he imagined. Plus his late work hours helped to reinforce this notion. Yet he enjoyed making house calls, as he was now. It allowed him to spy on the lairs of other creatures. He was fascinated by their habitats, how they were decorated, the conditions, noting the furniture (made from woven-straw), the rock walls (polished to a sheen), and the dirt floor (neatly swept). It was a humble abode, yet charming nonetheless. A fire glowed in a hearth and was keeping them all warm.

"Am I here to harm you? Not at all." Owen set down a leather bag which he unclasped at the top. Removing a stethoscope and then a tongue depressor, he said, "Might I have a look and a listen, little fellow? It will not hurt."

As usual, it would be the smallest who was sick, forehead damp from fever. They were often the first to succumb to ill health during these early stages of growth. Oddly, they had a tendency to flourish once they survived, even outgrow their siblings. He found this odd. Existence, itself, he found to be, well, *odd*.

"Do you have a name?"

The little mouse was quivering uncontrollably.

His mother prodded, speaking for him. "Martin?"

"*Martin*," echoed Owen, "we've done this before. Remember? Can I get you to open your mouth wide... and tell me... what?"

"*Auhhhh...*"

"That's good boy. Ah, as I suspected, your tonsils are inflamed. Not to worry. I will let you *keep* them." With a wink and a hearty chuckle, he said, "Now allow me to hear your chest."

His patient unbuttoned his pajama top, flinching only slightly when the cold metal diaphragm touched his fuzzy skin.

The boy spoke tentatively, "What... is wrong with me?"

Owen perked with amusement. "Well, I would say you are *sick*. It happens to us all. You have a fever. You caught a little bug."

"A bug?"

"Wee little things," said the doctor, returning his medical tools to his leather bag. "Smaller than you. They come and go, vacationing inside us peacefully. But now and then we become the host to unruly guests – nasty bugs – who create havoc and bully us, thinking they can overtake our bodies. They give us a scare. But I am certain you will prevail. And be yourself, feeling better, very soon."

Owen stood and fluffed his coat of feathers in preparation for his departure. He retrieved his dangling monocle hung on a string and attached the glass to his face. "My third eye," he joked, and gave a wink, eyeing once again this lovely morsel (*mother*) before tipping his head toward her. "Madam."

Cheeks blushing, she opened the door to her children's bedroom, then shut it quietly behind them as they walked back into the living room where she paused. The moment became awkward.

"Doctor, you're my savior. I can't thank you enough for coming. Being a widow left all alone to raise five children, I get worried sick. I'm sorry you came all this way for nothing. I was afraid my little Martin... he... forgive me, I am such a *fool.*"

Owen came to aid this pretty mouse by entering her personal space, to deftly take hold of her delicate hand and tell her, "You are *not* a fool. You are a good mother to worry."

"Doctor—"

"Call me Owen."

"May I offer you something to eat before you go?"

"Well, I..." Owen fought back his inner demons. She had whet his appetite. His mouth was watering. He hungered for a taste of what this delectable woman had to offer, yet he knew he shouldn't, and therefore smiled, able to keep his desires in check and see her as a platonic kindred spirit. "A tempting offer, Madam, but—"

"Please, Owen, call me Sarah."

"Sarah, thank you. But I must decline."

"I understand."

The disappointment on her face made him reconsider. He shut one eye to peer like a cyclops through his other, before removing his monocle and tucking it into his breast pocket. He could see she was a woman in need of special healing. It was his calling. And she was calling him to give into his urges and heal her.

What followed was a passionate consensual impromptu tussle of uninhibited passion that bound them into a whirling cyclone force, bumping into cabinets and walls and doorways, until they collapsed intertwined upon a bedroom mattress. Then Owen's inner demons arrived as if out of nowhere to attack his mind, seeking dominance.

Heroically he fought back and broke from the reins of his primordial instincts. He succeeded in restraining his savage impulse to devour her by sublimating his transgressions and transfering the urge into an erotic nibbling and poking of her luscious body from head to toe. The mouse squealed with pleasure in a startled measure of terror and delight. When it was all over, they both lay sighing, exhausted, side by side. Owen pecked her with a goodbye kiss.

Flying back through the dead of night to his office, Owen was second-guessing his decision to do what he had done. He was able to rationalize to himself that (technically) she was not his patient (at that moment). But had his actions violated the Hippocratic Oath? So lost in thought he could no longer tell if it was day or night. It seemed he was always in a rush to be somewhere. He glanced down imagining the dreams of others as he flew. These worlds of slumber were as nebulous as the mist he witnessed glowing upon the horizon. Daybreak and twilight seemed indistinguishable. He wished to close his eyes but resisted.

As the dark woods and sleeping town passed beneath his wings he began thinking about the rumors he had been overhearing all day. Snippets of gossip, whispered conversations from those waiting in his reception room. One patient even voiced these concerns directly to him while he examined her.

The gist of it was: A gigantic little girl had entered Evolsdog.

Gigantic? Little? It was oxymoronic. Both could not be true! A girl? A human? Impossible! It was against all the rules. And yet, as a doctor, a practitioner of the healing arts, abnormalities did exist. Nature was full of mischief. He had once seen a two-headed snake. Who knows, maybe there existed two of him? Another Owen Owl hooting through the early morning fog, but unlike himself, weaving through a congestion of traffic – braking and accelerating – trying to arrive on time at a prestigious medical clinic.

Ensconced in his office chair and half asleep, half awake, he was warming his hands on a styrofoam cup of coffee. He was scheduled to perform surgery in an hour. He was reviewing the procedure in his head and assessing the likely outcome of his patient – the odds of recovery versus to never wake again. Measuring his sips through the punctured lid of the container, Owen tasted his responsibility. The weight of it all. The uncertainty. How unpredictable his power was over life and death. Untenable. Yet... held in his capable hands.

A frantic knocking caused Owen to lurch, having dozed, waking and knocking over something. He watched coffee spread like an oil spill, a blood stain, an infestation, ruining papers upon his desk.

"Who is it? Come in!"

For a moment, Owen distrusted where he was, what he was, and who these people were. The rabbit, he recalled, had represented him in court. The beaver he knew from his weekly poker night. But why was the Prime Minister in his office? And the others? A crow and frog were carrying a colorfully limp body and were about to place it upon his desk. He steered them toward an examination table.

The rumors were true. Partially. It *was* a girl. But she was not gigantic. Instead, quite tiny. But relative to who and what?

He asked, "What is the meaning of this? Who—"

"I found her in a meadow," said Wyatt. "Early this morning."

"She fell from the sky," said Hazel.

"She what!?" said Owen.

"Like a blazing comet!" said Riley.

"That," said Owen, "is scientifically not possible."

"Mysterious, yet," said Wick, touching her leg with the tip of his cane. "And she insists on calling herself a *cat*."

Wyatt pushed the cane aside. "She only calls herself Kat."

Owen blinked his bloodshot eyes. "This is exceedingly complex. So you are saying she has *not* been in this state the entire time?"

"No," said Wyatt, "but unconscious when I found her."

"In the meadow?" Owen reached for his eye scope.

"Yes, where she awoke," clarified Wyatt, "and remained awake until this afternoon when she lost consciousnesss again."

"Like someone yanked out her dang plug," said Izzy.

Harold tapped his notepad, preparing to write. "Losing power. Falling flat on her face. I have it all written here in my notes."

"Well that would explain the mud," said Owen.

"Chocolate," said Scarlet.

"Chocolate?" Owen touched the leather fringe on her jacket.

Izzy unsheathed his knife. "She ain't fit to be here. Care to use this on her, Doc?"

"Put that away," said Owen. "She came dressed like this?"

"That was Camille's doing," said Hazel.

"Camille?" Owen examined Kat's limp wrist.

"You know her, that *chameleon*," said Riley.

"Oh, yes, I've seen her around," mused Owen. "Another oddity. I suppose it's time to find out if this girl is alive."

The group assembled around Kat's supine body.

"Ah!" Owen pronounced. "She has a pulse!"

"Hallelujah!" said Hazel.

"But a faint one," added Owen. He peeled back the lid of Kat's right eye to peek inside, peering through his scope. "Hum... *odd*."

"What is it?" said Wyatt.

Owen examined Kat's other eye. "Have a look yourself."

They all jostled to nudge closer for a look.

Owen displayed her blue eyes by holding up both lids. "See how big and almost... well, *feline* they are."

"As I predicted," said Scarlet. "It has begun."

Wyatt leaned in close. "Her eyes look the same as before."

"Who knows?" Owen hooted. "She might *be* a cat!"

Kat became cognizant she was surrounded by animals. She had regained consciousness, but remained still. She peripherally caught glimpses of disturbing images – photographs, charts, illustrations –

hung upon the walls. They depicted bodies in states of evisceration and dissection.

Kat pushed the owl away. "Take your hands off me!"

Alarmed, Owen stumbled back, dropping his magnifying glass. It shattered upon the floor. "God-Almighty! She can talk!"

"Of course I can *talk*," said Kat, attempting to sit up. She was feeling woozy. A frog helped steady her. "Where am I?"

"Same place as before," said Wyatt. "Welcome back."

"Oh, hi. What happened? Why am I—"

"You passed out, dear," said Hazel.

"Face first into a plate of chocolates," said Harold.

Kat touched her chin, licking her fingers. "I remember."

"Ah, a good sign," noted Owen. "How *many* did you eat?"

"I don't recall," said Kat.

Harold grunted, taking notes, "You do *not* recall. Uh, huh, how many times have I heard *that* line of defense before?"

"I don't feel very good." Kat sat up, looked at herself, touching the green beaded dress, the harlequin tights, the fringe that dangled from her jacket, then the acorn necklace.

"Which brings us back to *me*," beamed Owen. "The reason you were brought to my office. For me to examine you. Abnormalities force the mind to examine normality."

"Who *are* you?"

"*Who*—indeed! I am a physician. Doctor Owl."

"You look like an owl," said Kat.

"You would not be the first to make that comparison."

"What happened to Camille?"

"Your new friend dropped you like a bad habit," said Scarlet.

"She was nice to me," defended Kat. "I mean… sorta."

Scarlet touched the hem of Kat's short dress. "And look what she has turned you into. A little tart."

"I am not a tart! What about you?"

"This is not about me," said Scarlet. "You're the one who keeps dropping from the sky. And falling on your face."

Owen scowled. "Signs of bad medicine or bad behavior. Don't go making it a habit. What else have you dropped? Besides making me *drop* my magnifying instrument!?"

"I'm sorry." Kat looked around. "What are you writing?"

Harold tapped his book. "Notes for your defense."

"Defense for what?"

"Against those who plan to prosecute you," said Harold.

"For the crimes you have committed," said Riley.

"But I haven't committed—"

"Making a spectacle of yourself?" said Scarlet.

"When?"

"Standing on your head in public is *illegal*," said Wick.

"How was I to know that?" said Kat.

"Ignorance of the law is no excuse," said Harold.

"But I'm not *from* here!" protested Kat.

"Egad!" Harold scribbled more notes. "Hold your tongue. This is in no way helping your case."

"My case?" said Kat.

"For your upcoming trial," said Wick.

"Am I being arrested?" said Kat.

"No," said Riley, "I did that already."

"Are you taking me to jail?"

"Done that," said Riley. "Been there."

"Look on the bright side," said Damian. "The entire town is looking forward to your tribunal."

Kat looked at Wyatt. "I thought you said you'd help me get back home. I don't understand what's happening."

Wyatt brought a finger to his lips to silence her while Hazel gave her legs a light dusting.

Harold closed his notebook. "This is not adding up at all."

Wick fingered his medallion to call attention to his authority as the Prime Minister and told her, "Once the doctor pronounces you *fit* to stand trial, we shall proceed posthaste to the proceedings."

"Straight to court!" said Damian.

"To court?" Kat swung her legs and hung them off the table.

Damian slapped himself. "*Courtyard!* Not a court, per se. And not far from here."

"And everyone," said Scarlet, circling Kat, "is expecting you to make an appearance."

"Who is everyone?" said Kat.

"The court of public opinion," said Wick.

"It's a kangaroo court," said Harold.

"Kangaroo?" said Kat.

"*Iguana*," said Riley, "before that stupid kangaroo."

"He retired," said Wick.

"Did *not*," said Izzy. "He went bonkers!"

"This is *crazy*," said Kat.

"He agreed!" said Wick. "Arriving at the same conclusion."

"Who?" said Kat.

"Our ex-judge," said Wick. "But that is here nor there. You see, whichever way, it all works in *my* favor. Damian, my assistant here, has conducted a survey to poll the results of your popularity. It will determine your fate. You see, it is not up to *me* to decide. Therefore, you see, there is no way *I* can lose."

Kat's confusion turned to anger. "But what about *me!?*

"You?" said Wick. "This doesn't concern you."

Kat shouted, "What do you *mean* it doesn't concern me!?"

"He means," explained Riley, "the outcome is predetermined. Your fate is sealed."

"Your goose is crook'd," said Izzy.

"*Cooked*," Wyatt corrected. "The expression is—"

"If I say her goose is a *crook*," growled Izzy, "then he is!"

"I don't *have* a goose!" said Kat.

"*That*," said Harold, "is what we are going to determine."

"Please, all I want to do is go home," pleaded Kat.

"Good for you," said Hazel. "Good manners will get you far. And remember to keep listening to your nut."

Kat forgot she was wearing a pendant and looked down at the crystal acorn.

"In the end," Harold said, "we all return to where we started. You broke the law coming here, as you are, looking like that. Not good, no good at all."

Kat shook her head. "I have no idea what you're talking about. Or how your crazy world works."

"Do you wish to hire my services?

"Not really. What good would you be to me?"

"No good at all," said Harold. "But as good as you get. In fact, I am very good at everything I do."

"Which is what—*nothing?*" Kat hopped off the table.

"Now see here, young lady!" Harold took offense and gave his ears a cursory scratch before flinging them backwards. "I specialize in doing *nothing* and have prospered quite well at doing *nothing*, thank-you-very-much. You should see the size of my house. In fact, I've written a manifesto on the very subject of... well, nothing!"

"Rats are fat," said Izzy. "Ya can't dispute that. Like I told ya, I built the power grid that runs this place. I know how things work around these parts. But as far as eyes concede, I can't see what part you is fixin' to play."

Owen intervened to ask Kat, "Are you feeling any better?"

Kat realized she was. "I think I am. Yes, thank you."

"The girl is healed!" screeched Owen. "My work is done!"

"Splendid," said Wick. "Off to court!"

"*Yard*," stressed Damian. "Courtyard. A grove, technically." He was stationed at a door and opened it ceremoniously to reveal a darkening sky and a large deck lit with strings of light.

The twilight confused Owen. "Where do all the days go?"

Damian clapped his hands sharply to gain the room's attention before marching out the door through a horde of animals mulling around drinking cocktails and eating appetizers. He was internally giddy, yet showed not a trace of emotion, relishing the hidden reins of power he held, unbeknownst to the masses, including Wick. He knew precisely how to rouse and manipulate a crowd, going straight for the central support post at the center of the deck which housed a bronze bell. His demeanor, which displayed a subordinate lack of ambition, was belied by how forcefully he yanked on the clanger.

Unemotionally, he cried out, "Let the ceremony begin!"

Riley prodded Kat toward the door. "Keep in mind, I am here to protect you from the throng of citizenry waiting to tear you limb from limb – *if* you try to resist me."

Alarmed, Kat asked, "Why would they do that?"

Riley laughed, "How should I know? They may toss flowers."

The frog hopped ahead of the crow to block the way.

"Don't do this, Riley," said Wyatt. "You're better than this."

"I am really not." Riley pushed Wyatt aside.

Izzy pointed his knife at Wyatt. "Ya can't stop the unstoppable. So stay out of this—ya turncoat toad!"

Wyatt backed out the door. "Don't call me that!"

Kat was pushed out next and said, "He's actually a tree frog."

"So—*not* an artist?" Riley laughed, enjoying himself, especially the attention, as he herded his prisoner along.

The beaver spit on a flat stone he held, grinding his blade.

"Izzy," said Riley. "These artists, they modify and falsify reality. No one admits to being one unless they are hiding something."

Izzy took aim and flung his knife, sticking the blade into the knot of a redwood. "Ya hit the bull right in its eye, Riley."

Kat realized they were no longer in the village but somewhere up the mountain. Situated in the redwoods, the deck looked out on the upper branches of a tree. Like the perch of an owl's nest, except for how expansive it was, resembling a resort, or a lodge. Animals were socializing, engaged in conversation, but stopped talking to watch her pass.

Her entourage consisted of Izzy, Wick and Owen leading the way, with Riley and Wyatt on opposite sides of her, then Scarlet, Harold, Hazel and Damian trailing. Izzy hustled ahead to yank from the trunk of a redwood his knife. Wick gave facile waves and paused along the way to shake hands. Owen eyed the appetizers on plates and spotted several delectable rodents and bugs he desired to eat but kept moving along the straight-and-narrow path.

Kat was overhearing snippets of comments from the crowd as she passed:

"Who does she think she is?"

"She's guilty, all right. Guilty of trespassing."

"Coming here looking like that."

"I can't wait to see how this plays out tonight."

"The prosecution has built a solid case."

"He's a clever prosecutor."

"Prosecutor?" said Kat. "Who? I haven't even met—"

"That would be me," said Harold, who turned his head and wagged his tiny notebook at her.

"But you said you would *defend* me," said Kat.

"Ah, yes, well," said Harold, raising his nose to sniff and dismiss a foul odor. "That was before you *terminated* my services."

"This isn't fair," said Kat.

Riley swiped at a reporter who got too close. "Nor is life. And death? – that's just the flipside. Not as good as side A, some say, but side B can often surprise." The crow then shoved aside a porcupine – pushing his camera to avoid being poked by his barbed quills.

Kat leaned toward Wyatt to say, "I'm afraid. Should I be?"

"Yes!" said Riley. "Fear keeps you alive."

"Thanks," said Kat sarcastically, "for being my *friend*."

"Don't mention it," said Riley.

"Stay focused," Wyatt advised. "And try to stay calm."

"You keep saying that. It's not helping."

Having moved off the deck, Kat was now being escorted down a path buttressed on both sides by tall bushes sculpted into walls.

"What happens if they decide I'm guilty?"

From behind her, Damian said neutrally, "We put you to bed."

"To bed?"

Damian slapped his face, chastising himself. "*Sleep!* I meant. Civilized by other standards. We used to shoot or hang the accused. You'll find that our judicial system has become rather... peaceful."

"Not at all unreasonable," said Wick. "Democratic, as a rule. Plus, I can't be held accountable. In fact, I'm washing my hands of the entire matter. See? You are *out* of my hands. Poof!"

"I don't want to die," said Kat.

Owen rotated his head toward her with his monocle magnifying his one eye. Catching light, the lens turned opaque. "The transition *fascinates* me. You will find it is not all bad being placed under fire. Each crucible is a measure to purify your character."

Wyatt whispered in her ear, "Don't let any of this scare you."

"Too late," said Kat.

They emerged from the tunnel of shrubbery onto a path leading down into a grove of ancient redwoods. At the center was a stage, circular with footlights spanning its circumference, illuminating two performers. The stage was surrounded by long tables branching out in rows like beams from the sun with illuminated lights strung out, spanning and interlacing the neighboring redwoods which had lights spiraling around the trunks. Tables were filled to capacity with all varieties of animals dining and laughing at the antics taking place on stage as waiters and waitresses moved up and down the aisles taking orders and serving meals.

"*This* is the court?" asked Kat. "Where my trial will be?"

Wick stopped on the knoll in admiration. "It is."

"It's a dinner theater!"

"We like to keep our legal system entertaining." Wick removed his top hat and waved at the horde of animals assembled below. No one seemed to notice. Wick donned his hat. "They will love me for providing you to them. These festivities will boost my popularity. Especially with *you* as the star attraction."

"Wow, I feel so *special*," said Kat.

"Watch your attitude," cautioned Hazel. "The audience will not take kindly to a new arrival who acts snippety."

Kat's entourage began to move her again, winding down a trail. As they approached the entrance to this outdoor arena, Wyatt leaped in front to make another appeal.

"Stop! These proceedings have no legitimacy. We don't have the right to judge whether she can stay or not. It's premature."

Damian said, "I have—I *mean*." He slapped himself sharply. "*He* has the right. The Prime Minister!"

"But she is already *here*," said Wyatt. "That counts for—"

"Good point," said Harold, "I propose *you* defend her."

"I'm an artist," said Wyatt. "A painter of nature's wonders – not a criminal attorney!"

"Ha!" cawed Riley. "We grant you artistic license to perform due process. *Do* proceed, counselor. Ha!"

"Will you help me?" asked Kat.

"I might be your only choice," said Wyatt.

"It could be worse," said Riley.

"Let *me* represent you," said Izzy.

"No thanks," said Kat.

"Then you accept the challenge?" stated Harold.

"Wyatt will," said Hazel. "Won't you?" She turned to reassure

Kat by saying, "Don't you worry. Wyatt will think of something. Did I tell you, he once saved my life? Everyone thought I was nuts! So I had to convince them I was! Can you imagine?"

Kat smiled politely at the squirrel as she chattered with laughter. Kat realized she was in deep trouble.

From the audience there was hooting and clapping and laughing as Kat passed down the main aisle. She felt like a reluctant bride, receiving many heads to turn and ogle and gasp. She avoided these hungry eyes by looking straight ahead. She belatedly focused on the stage and realized she was looking at a donkey and elephant juggling swords and flaming torches – comically hurling them aggressively back and forth faster and faster.

"Someone's going to get hurt!"

"Isn't that the point?"

The crowd responded to the shout-and-reply with applause.

Kat's eyes strayed from the stage to glance over the sea of tables – at the animals dining, the waiters serving – and noticed several seals in tuxedos moving up and down the aisles. They were brandishing leaflets and barking, "Cast your vote! Who hasn't voted? Buy three and you get one free!"

"They're selling votes?" said Kat.

"Calm down," said Wyatt.

"Don't tell me to calm down!" said Kat.

"No one ever bothers to count them," said Hazel.

"But this is my life! How can they not—"

Kat stopped when someone bumped into her from behind.

Riley yanked her by the arm. "Keep moving."

Kat pointed at protesters near the stage holding up placards with clashing messages that were bobbing in the air:

KILL THE CAT! SAVE THE CAT! KILL THE CAT!

"Are they talking about me?" said Kat.

"Well—*whooo*—else would it be?" hooted Owen, excited by the frenzy and waving back.

"You are the *talk* of the town," said Hazel.

"I should be jealous," said Scarlet. "Yet I predict your star will be shooting and dying soon. So I need not be."

Kat was distracted next by a coyote carrying a concession stand hanging by straps from his shoulders. He was shouting:

"Place your bets! Who hasn't placed their bet?"

The coyote collided into their moving entourage.

"Still time to place your—*you*—it's you! You're *her!*"

Both Kat and coyote became speechless, gawking at each other.

The coyote recovered to say, "Care to wager a bet?"

"On whether I *live* or die?"

"Very good odds." The coyote grinned. "Five to one you'll die. Bet on *yourself* and you could win big! *If* you live."

Kat kicked him in the shin.

The coyote howled and the crowd roared with laughter.

Limping in her ballet slippers, her toe now sore from the kicking, Kat was led to a reserved table by the stage and told by Riley to sit. Her group took seats on the bench around her.

"Feast your eyes on the crowd!" said Wick, looking around with nervous excitement, straightening his medal. He saw a microphone, completely alone, unattended, on its stand at the center of the stage. Wick felt the pull, as though from a magnet. "I must say something! Something *important.*"

His assistant pulled him back down. "Not now, Sir."

"If not *now* when?"

"Once I—" Damian slapped himself. "*You* think of something worthy to say to the crowd. Give me a moment to think for you."

"Don't think too long," said Wick impatiently.

"When is my trial supposed to start?" asked Kat.

"Right after the Rodéo Pigs." Riley handed her a program. "Best of Show is coming up next."

"What's that?"

"Bluebloods," said Hazel.

"The pure breeds." Riley flipped back his goggles to roll his eyes at her from beneath his dark brows. "Old guard hoity-toity stuff."

"It's a beauty pageant, really," said Scarlet, "for those who claim to be connected by a traceable lineage."

Riley added, "It's *pure—*"

"*Bollocks,*" said Izzy. "I prefer those upstarts. Those pigs ain't afraid to get dirty. Now that's entertainment. Pure and simple."

"You're on after them," said Hazel, pointing. "It says so right here. See? That's you. Case of the Fallen Cat."

"But I'm *not* a cat," said Kat.

"We shall see about *that,*" said Harold.

"The fact that you *are* a little girl," said Wyatt, "and *not* a cat is the reason for this whole mess."

"Why, look," said Scarlet, "you have fans."

Seated at a table a few rows away, Kat noticed a group of rowdy cats – cougars, leopards, panthers – staring at her lasciviously. One gave her a sly wink and a lewd grin.

Scarlet added, "Who knows, you might get lucky tonight."

"Want do they want?"

"You have to ask?"

Kat's alarm was escalating. Everywhere she looked animals were staring back. "What are you saying? All of this is happening because I'm a girl. No one would even care if I *was* a cat?"

Scarlet laughed. "I doubt that."

"I might care," said Hazel.

Scarlet countered, "It is unbefitting to care. Be yourself."

Kat glanced up to see animals now parading about on the stage, segregated by species — spider monkeys, great danes, polar bears.

"Wait 'till ya see them pigs," said Izzy, giving Kat a nudge. "Pork is a tough act to follow. See all that? Up there. That's my doing."

"You mean the lights?"

"Magic." Izzy combed his whiskers and mysteriously squinted as if to conceal his powers. He tapped his sharp forefinger on a dinner plate. "Illumination! With all that water I turn night into daylight. Impressive, eh? I can do it with wind too."

"Electricity," said Kat.

Izzy blinked rapidly. "What'd ya say?"

"You're generating an electrical current?"

"Wrong!" said Izzy. "I harness and transform nature!"

"Does your magic involve metal? Coils of wire? Rotation?"

Izzy slammed his fists on the table and his tail upon the ground – startling everyone. "Who you been talking to!? Huh? Angelo?"

"Angelo?"

"*Dam* lizard." Izzy spit into a cup. "Has to be. Spilling the bees about my trade secrets! Traitor!"

"Electricity," said Kat. "It's... like capturing lightning."

Izzy slammed his palm. "There she goes again!"

"Calm down," said Wyatt, turning from the stage. "What's the problem now?"

"*She* is the problem!" Izzy clawed the wood with his fingernails. "She ain't supposed to know nothing about what I knows—but she knows! Somehow. How do ya?"

"I learned about electricity in school," said Kat innocently.

"No way! That low-life *lizard* told ya. Didn't he!?"

"I don't know any lizard!" Kat shouted back.

Izzy drew a knife from his holster and stabbed the blade in the table, shaking the dishes. "I vote yes!"

"Which means what?" said Kat.

"For putting you to *sleep*. Permanently. Sound harsh?"

"Yes," said Kat, taken aback. "You want me to die?"

"Harrumph," said Izzy. "You know *less* than I thought."

Kat looked but nobody seemed concerned about their heated

exchange. Everyone was focused on the stage where a new act was beginning. She had lost track of time. She took a program off the table and read its cover. HIGH JINKS. Several pigs dressed in suits, others in formal gowns, were descending upon a platform by ropes through a hole into what resembled an enormous fishbowl partially filled with brown sludge.

Kat asked Wyatt. "What are they doing?"

"Hoping to get filthy rich."

"Is that mud?"

"Mixed with beans, pond slime, and who knows what else."

"*Auhg,* it smells awful." Kat covered her nose.

"A reality game intended to ward off boredom."

Kat watched as the pigs emersed themselves up to their waist and necks in the muck. Then a whistle blew and they began to wrestle. Fighting off rivals, they broke free – plunging beneath the surface of sludge, coming up for air, then diving back down again.

The crowd was screaming out names and shouting.

"What are they diving for?"

"You'll see," said Wyatt

Several pigs surfaced clutching a crystal globe covered in filth. Each fighting to take possession of this slick ball, they all sludged communally, arms locked around the orb, toward an elevated hoop. Amidst elbowing and head butting, one pig pried the ball loose from the others and tossed it through the hoop.

The redwood grove exploded with roars and whistles.

"What happened?" asked Kat.

Wyatt feigned enthusiasm, then tilted his head toward Kat so she could hear. "It's called winning. The other competitors, the losers, submit to licking the ball clean as part of a ceremonial succession to the victor."

"That's disgusting." Kat winced as she watched.

"No harm, no foul," said Wyatt. "A popular sport among the

populus. It's to see how low a soul will sink to gain these earthly spoils. Entertainment by another name. By the way, we're on next. Are you ready?"

"Ready for what? What's supposed to happen?"

"Stay calm. Pretend you're having fun. That helps."

Kat saw Wick emerge from the wings of the stage. She glanced at his empty seat (not realizing he had left) to make sure there were not duplicates of this weasel roaming about.

Wick tapped the microphone to confirm it was amplified.

"Good evening, my friends! Are you ready for the main event? Ready to embrace the spirit of nonpartisanship? To reach across the aisle and work harmoniously with those who hold opposing views? To arrive at a compromise. Despite two *extremely* polarized camps. Kill the cat? Save the cat? How do we settle this spat? How can we reach the middle where common ground is found? Well, I say, it is elementary. Quite simple. We *skin* the cat!"

Wick grinned, enjoying the outburst he provoked – the derisive snorts of laughter and howls of merriment. He waved his short arms to placate and silence the audience.

"Tonight will be special. I am pleased to introduce a brand new attraction. An unexpected guest. If you have read your programs, heard the rumors, possibly seen this *anomaly* yourself, then you know we have a miniature girl among us. A rarity. Who claims to have fallen from the sky! Or, to be precise, her *defendant* claims to have seen her fall. None other than Wyatt T. Frog. Our resident daydreamer. A painter of nature's *wonders*. An artist, by profession. Or so he *professes*. Ah, but can he illustrate for us the true meaning of *this* perplexing wonder, I wonder? Hum?"

A spatter of laughter followed.

"So, tonight, Wyatt will be pleading her case, playing the part of an *attorney*. Attempting to explain the inexplicable. Defending an unfortunate little girl who has lost her way. Yet wishes to stay."

"I never said that," said Kat.

"*Shssssh*," Wyatt counseled her. "Play along."

"Stay!?" repeated Wick, pausing for emphasis. "Here?" Lifting his top hat he pointed with his cane toward Kat for theatrical effect. "We have *rules* of order. Proper conduct to adhere to. And, as your elected representative, I uphold them! I hold firm to our core values! While remaining neutral. With no horse in this race to bet on. No slice of bread to spread my butter upon. Not a pot to—well, you get the idea. I needn't be right, nor wrong. I am a leader, not a divider. Not even a decider. It shall fall upon *you* to decide whether she is banished or if she is to stay. Your collective wisdom, based on biased ideologies and hearsay, will decide her fate. It will be a testament to this ambiguous union of self-governance, a pledge of allegiance to our independently-minded democratic republic! Which constitutes our absolute blind faith in this celestial island state!"

A banner dropped from the redwoods that spanned the stage:

VOTE WICK: HE BURNS FOR YOU AT BOTH ENDS

"You will therefore have no one else to blame except yourselves if you fail to succeed in determining the correct outcome in this case. Which I trust you will *all* remember – when casting your vote for *me* come election day!"

As the banner lifted back into the darkness, Wick proclaimed, "But enough of *me*. Personally, I've had enough of myself and all the mud-slinging I've had to endure while presiding here."

"Four more years!" someone heckled, followed by laughter.

"Yes, well, without further adieu—let the *trial* begin!"

Wild applause burst from the audience. Alarming Kat who was lifted by her arms from her seat by Riley and Izzy. They escorted her onto the stage, followed by Harold and Wyatt. On opposite sides of a towering monolithic bench were two opposing tables with chairs, each on a dais. At center stage, between both tables and bench, was a red upholstered seat elevated like a throne with three tiny steps.

Riley nudged her toward it, indicating she take the stand.

Once seated, Kat looked out upon the sparkling lights and sea of animals dining beneath the redwoods. She was terrified.

Wyatt approached to whisper in her ear, "Relax."

"Stop saying that," she said back. "It's really not helping."

"*Calm* down," advised Wyatt. "I'll be right over there."

Wyatt hopped over to the table on her left where Hazel was busy dusting it thoroughly, along with each chair, before taking a seat. Hazel sat beside him. At the opposite table sat Harold scratching in his notebook with a pen while Scarlet stroked his ears, holding them up so they wouldn't flop down into his line of vision. On either side of the bench stood Riley and Izzy to officiate as officers of the law for this judicial proceeding.

"All rise!" shouted Riley.

Kat stood with everyone else on stage. The audience stood too. She was surprised to see – expecting a kangaroo – the owl emerge to take the bench. The doctor was wearing a judge's robe.

There was an unsettled rumbling within the audience.

Izzy stepped forward to announce. "Shut up! Listen up! It's still gonna be a kangaroo court. Billy's under the weather, recouping after last night's fight. Ya all seen him take one heck of a walloping. He sends his regrets, says he ain't fit to judge tonight's proceeding. So disregard your programs. In his stead we got our own Doc Owen to fill in last minute. So *pipes* down! Enjoy the show before you blow a fuse in your heads!"

There was applause, murmurs, and a few hoots of laughter.

Owen adjusted his monocle, then tapped his gavel. "First case."

"We have only one," said Wyatt.

"Objection!" said Harold.

"On what grounds?" asked Owen.

"The prosecution gets to speak first. The defense is out of order. Wyatt should be fined."

"Fine," said Owen. "You owe me a drink. Proceed."

Harold stood, brushing back his ears. Approaching the bench, then turning on Kat, then the audience. "Look at her. We all know she shouldn't be here. It's a cut-and-dry case. As I will *prove* beyond any reason for anyone to doubt me that she is guilty! This creature, this... this little *girl* – who claims to be a cat – must be removed! Like an unsightly weed in our garden! Thank you."

The audience applauded, amidst random shouts wagering her guilt or innocence.

Wyatt pointed to himself for confirmation that it was his turn to get up and talk. He stood. "This girl is *not* guilty." He was about to sit but was repelled back by Hazel's knitted brow.

"That's it?" she accused. "Your *entire* opening remark?"

"No... I..."

"Are you now conceding she *is* guilty?" quipped Harold.

"Silence!" Owen was enjoying his role as judge and kept tapping his gavel forcefully until there was nothing heard but the pounding of wood upon wood. When he finally stopped, thrilled by the silence he provoked, he said, "*Now* you may proceed."

Wyatt had removed his beret, beginning to perspire, but resisted swiping the moisture from his face. "I wanted to add that I have come to know this girl, and I have found her to be quite delightful. She does not pose any threat to us. And she does not *think* she is a cat. Her *name* is Kat. She is merely looking to find her way home. Nor does she wish to be here."

"Then let's put her to sleep!" came a shout from the crowd.

"Silence!" Owen pointed. "Someone arrest that jackal! I want that menace thrown out of my courtroom immediately!"

Riley tapped the bench. Owen looked down at him.

"You don't have that authority," said Riley.

"Who does?"

The audience began chanting in rival choruses:

"Down... Down... Down..."

"Up... Up... Up..."

Owen pounded his gavel. "Enough! The girl will be put down when she is found guilty. Only then. Are you done?"

Wyatt held up a finger. "The girl is innocent. And I will prove that she is."

"Done now?" asked Owen.

"Yes," said Wyatt. "For now. Thank you."

"I believe the prosecution starts?" Owen rotated his head in both directions, asking no one in particular.

Harold squeezed Scarlet's hand for good luck then rose from his seat and took command. He came from behind the table holding his notebook. He wagged it at the audience, then at the defense, as if he held the defendant's confessions in his hand. Confidently he slapped the little book upon his open palm.

"I want you to tell the audience, little girl, who you are."

"My name is Kat. K. A. T. It's short for Kathlyn."

"Yes-yes, indeed," said Harold, gesturing grandly, hopping in small skips and steps about on stage. "We all can *see* you are quite short. But in no *way* do you physically resemble a cat!"

The audience laughed.

"I never said—"

"Speak only when asked to speak." Owen gave a gavel tap.

"Where do you come from?" asked Harold.

"I—"

"And *why* are you here? Answer that?"

"I don't really know why."

"Well then..." Harold expressed to the audience a theatrical air of suspicion. "What *do* you know? Anything?"

Kat looked at Wyatt, Owen, then Harold. "How am I supposed to answer that? I know a lot of things."

"Specifically," said Harold, rocking back on his heels.

"Can you be specific?" said Kat.

"Now see here!" Harold threw his book to the floor. "I asked you first! Judge? I need a ruling. Make her answer my question."

Owen blinked augustly. "Answer the question, little girl."

"Could you repeat the question?" said Kat.

Having forgotten, Harold scratched his ears. Glancing at Riley, he decided to improvise. "You came here as a *spy*, did you not?"

"No," said Kat.

"No? Riley Crow over there told me you—"

"He's wrong," said Kat.

"Let me finish!" Harold bent down and retrieved his notebook off the floor.

Owen tapped his gavel. "Do not interrupt, little girl."

"Kat," said Kat.

Owen peered at her and touched his third eye. "*That* has not been proven, as yet, has it? Learn to play by the rules. Or I will have you *ejected* from my courtroom!"

"You cannot," said Riley. "*She* is the one on trial."

Izzy clucked his tongue at Riley. "Dam stupid lizard. Why'd he have to go crazy and retire?"

"Did you wish to finish?" Owen asked Harold.

"I haven't even begun!" said Harold. He swiveled toward Kat. "If you did not come here as a spy, then *why* did you – and *how* did you – manage to get here? Who sent you?"

"You asked me three questions," said Kat.

"So answer them," said Harold.

"I don't know *why* or *how*. Or *who*. Honestly, I wish I knew."

Her remark threw Harold off course. "How are we supposed to get anywhere if you refuse to cooperate?"

"I am trying to cooperate," said Kat.

"Try harder." Harold consulted his notebook. "Twain Meadow. Why there? Did you fall through a matrix in the sky? A result of paranormal triangular activity? Are you part of a cult?"

"No," said Kat.

"No to which question?'

"All of them."

"Ah-ha!" Harold raised both arms, turning to face the audience. "Now she is telling us she did *not* fall from the sky!" He swiveled back at her. "Well *did* you or did you not?"

Kat pointed to Wyatt. "Ask him. He saw—"

"But I am asking *you!* The one who is under oath and who has been sworn to tell the truth and nothing but the—"

"But I was never sworn in," Kat interrupted.

Harold snorted, amused. "Then *why* should anyone believe what you have to say?"

Owen pounded his gavel. "Someone swear her in!"

Izzy rummaged through his tool belt, pulled out a page-worn manual to the power grid and held it out to Kat. "Touch it. Now ya swear ya won't be telling us any more lies?" said Izzy.

"But I haven't," said Kat, placing her hand of the manual.

"Ya swear?" said Izzy.

"I do," said Kat.

"That works for me." Izzy holstered his pamphlet.

"Does the prosecution rest?"

Harold was busy consulting with Scarlet, his back turned away from Owen. He swiveled around. "I will never rest until justice is served! I am a tireless advocate for—"

"Stop grandstanding. Get on with it already," said Owen.

Harold walked towards Kat, alternating between facing her and the restless audience. "I would like the defendant to tell us all *why* she was caught standing on her head."

"I didn't know it was illegal."

"That wasn't my question." Harold addressed Owen. "You see how she flaunts authority by refusing to answer. *You* are a witness."

"No, I am the judge," said Owen.

"Camille dared me to do it," said Kat.

"Camille, you say?" said Harold.

"The chameleon," said Kat. "I mean, if that is what she is."

"She *is* quite the chameleon. And why did she dare you to make a fool of yourself in public? Do you not *care* what others think of you? Socially? Do you not *care* if you fit in, and are accepted?"

Behind the rabbit Kat noticed the fox shaking her head.

"I believe I do," said Kat "I'm not sure."

"Not sure of what? That you will fit in here?"

"No," said Kat. "Camille bet me that if—"

"So you were *gambling!* Another offense. Now I've lost count!"

"She was going to show me how to get home if I won."

"I don't *care,*" said Harold. "The point is, you were gambling, cavorting in public, making a spectacle of yourself, and consuming chocolates. Plus – no minus – you were *drinking* in the street."

"We were at a sidewalk cafe," said Kat.

"Let's not *quibble* about details. Admit it. You lost the bet."

"I did," said Kat. "Which is the only reason I—"

"Lied?"

"No. Stood on my head."

"I see," said Harold, pacing in circles. "How did our world look to you upside down? Strike that. Let us circle back to the question I posed to you earlier."

Kat raised her hand straight up.

Harold stepped back, puzzled by her maneuver.

Kat looked up at the judge who was equally perplexed.

"Why is your arm raised?" asked Owen

"I think she means to surrender," said Harold.

"No," said Kat. "This is embarrassing. I need to use the little girl's room."

"We don't *have* a room for little girls," said Harold.

"I meant a *rest* room."

"You look rested," said Owen.

"A bathroom?"

"It's a trick," said Harold. "She was washed clean in the river."

Wyatt interjected. "A room where I can speak in private with my client. May we have a short recess, Your Honor?"

"I like the sound of that," said Owen. "Ask me again."

"If it pleases Your Honor, we would like a—"

"What for?" said Harold. "You can't call a time out! I had her up against the ropes. She was about to confess!"

"No she wasn't!" said Wyatt.

"—No I wasn't," said Kat in unison.

"I propose we vote now!" shouted Harold, playing to the crowd, gesturing for them to take a stand with him.

Many did, chanting, "*Kill the cat! Kill the cat!*"

Wyatt shouted, "The defense hasn't even presented its case!"

"Why waste your time?" said Harold. "Listen to the audience. Hear the jury? They have decided she is guilty as sin!"

"But I'm innocent!" Kat stood.

"Sit down!" warned Riley.

Scarlet was painting her long nails red at the prosecution table. "Little girl, you *lost* your innocence when you got lost in my palace. I will testify under oath you are no longer *pure*."

Kat blushed and sat down.

Wyatt approached the bench. "Your Honor. All I ask is for a few minutes to speak with my client. In private. It is permitted."

Owen twirled his gavel by its stem. "Very well. Case dismissed. No—I meant. What do I mean?"

"A short *recess*," hissed Riley.

"But no fooling around!" said Owen. "This is a court of *law* not a playground. We will reconvene in fifteen minutes."

Wyatt grabbed Kat's hand. "Come with me."

Riley was quick to follow, closely trailed by Izzy too.

"Where are we going?" said Kat.

"Don't you need to relieve yourself?"

"Not really," said Kat.

"Smart move."

"Are they going to hurt me? Or kill me if—"

"Listen," whispered Wyatt. "I have a plan."

They passed through a gauntlet of creatures who sought a closer look at this anomaly, many reaching into the aisle to touch her. They finally made it to the end of the aisle and past the dining area. Wyatt pulled her behind a cluster of huts which was the kitchen facility and brought her into an outdoor patio separated by a tall wooden fence. He closed the gate on Riley and Izzy.

He told them, "Give us some privacy."

"You have twelve more minutes," stated Riley.

"Don't waste your dime," said Izzy.

Wyatt moved Kat away from the fence and behind an ancient redwood. "It is my hope to get you out of this safely."

"Your hope!? You don't sound very sure of yourself."

Wyatt nodded toward the woods. "You need to go. Over there. Behind that grove of trees. There is an opening in the fence."

"I told you," said Kat. "I don't *have* to go."

"No—escape. There's a trail that leads up the mountain."

Kat didn't move. "That's your plan? You want me to run away? How does that help me? I mean, if I'm *there* instead of *here?*"

"There's a monastery. Our previous judge lives on the mountain. It's a retreat. A cavernous dwelling. A sanctuary. It's hard to miss."

"This judge will help me?"

"He used to be in charge, until he retired and threw it all away. He still has influence among this rabble. He's your best bet."

"You're not coming?"

"Who me? A silly frog?"

"I'm serious," said Kat. "Wyatt, I'm scared."

"I need to provide a diversion. Stall a mob from forming. Before they can figure out you've gone. I'll catch up later."

"You promise?"

"You'll be fine," said Wyatt.

"It's pitch dark," said Kat. "I don't even know—"

"Hazel found someone to guide you."

"Who?"

"Buzz. He's energetic. He has... qualities."

At the mention of his name, Kat sensed a soft whirring sound, a presence having snuck up behind her shoulder. She turned and was startled by a small head, the size of a child, with bulging black eyes. It was hovering so close she was distracted by the spikey antennae sprouting and bobbing in opposite directions in the air, before she noticed this creature had a wide grin.

"You're *her*. I'm Buster. Call me Buzz. It's what my friends call me. For my sound. *Buzzzzz*. Onomatopoeia. Get it?"

"I got it." Kat stepped back. "The name imitates your sound."

"You're smart." Buzz spoke rapid-fast pivoting toward Wyatt. "She's smart—quick—sharp."

"I'm Kat."

"I know that. Who doesn't? Everyone knows by now. But not a cat. Not a real cat. Are you friendly? You want to be my friend? I can be friendly. I'm helpful to have around. *See—look!*"

Kat hadn't realized there was more to his body – mostly a blur, invisible in the darkness. His rear end glowed yellow.

"Turn that thing off!" hushed Wyatt.

The firefly's abdomen went dark. "Sorry. I'm a show-off. Can't help myself. Nor can you. Being yourself. Who you are. Which is why you stick out. Out of place. A world of trouble. I can relate. I can. You need a guide. You need me. You remind me of someone. I like your fringe and shiny beads."

"Thanks." Kat backed away a notch.

Buzz hovered in. "Where are we going? Are we leaving now?"

"Yes," said Wyatt. "First, give her the coat."

Buzz zoomed away, was back in a flash, holding the garment in his mouth. Wyatt took it.

"It's one of Hazel's. This will keep you hidden. And warm."

Wyatt helped Kat put on the coat. It came to her ankles and was made of dark wool. It had a hood that covered her head.

"You look good," said Buzz. "Like a monk. Or a monkey. You could be anything. No one will know what. That's the idea."

"Take her to Angelo's place," said Wyatt.

"Angelo's? But that's through the webbed woods!" Buzz buzzed, informing Kat, "Spider webs. Riddled with spiders. I hate riddles. Mostly spiders. Not that I'm prejudiced. I like everyone. But—"

Wyatt added, "And stay away from the Poison Oak Pub!"

Buzz dipped his head. "You can trust me. I will. I mean I won't. I learned my lesson. I swear. Nope. No more going there."

"What's there?" said Kat.

"There is no there, *there*," said Buzz. "Not when you're *there*. You're elsewhere. No telling where. Difficult to tell."

"Go!" said Wyatt, prodding them both.

"Okay—be quick," said Buzz. "Follow my moves."

Wyatt touched her shoulder, "I'll be along as soon as I can."

Kat hurried to follow the motions of this unlit bug.

Once behind the crack in the fence, Kat was accosted by Buzz's head again. He moved close to buzz in her ear. "I'll light up once we get up the trail. Move your butt. Stay close. Follow my rear."

As he flew off, Kat muttered to herself, "Great. Now I'm taking orders from a bug."

chapter ten

Zhena Spider

Zhena Spider sensed the intruders coming in vibrations from the dark corners of her mind. Or, more precisely, from staring into the illuminating depths of her crystal egg. An opaque sterile orb that never hatched life. It lay in a nest of silk. Regardless of how flawed these visions sometimes turned out to be, she kept consulting it. She believed the ball revealed the future.

The little girl was with a firefly. They were traversing the woods, emerging from the grove. From this valley of darkness they passed by dwellings set back off the path. Other structures were perched on canyon walls. There were sounds of random activity. The comings and goings of strangers. Lights flickered between the redwoods on the hills. Below was a lake reflecting the moonlight. The pool of water kept getting progressively smaller.

Kat was enchanted. These distant dwellings resembled lanterns. The forest felt magical. Along this winding path solitary travelers would pass and nod at her hooded presence, while others, emersed in conversation, barely took notice of her dark cloistered shape or the light of her flittering companion.

Buzz flew close to her face. "Did you say something?"

"No," said Kat. "I'm just following your lead, Tinkerbell."

"Tinker-who? I'm not a bell. Do I look like a bell?"

Hovering eye level with her, Buzz glanced at his lit bottom. "Do you think I'm fat? Does my butt look too big to you?"

Kat swatted the air. "You're too close again. And I don't know what size your butt is supposed to be. It looks fine to me."

Buzz glowed brighter. "I like your butt too."

"Great. I'm glad we got that settled."

Kat's mood had soured. Having been thrust into the spotlit glare of so much attention, her life toyed with for the sake of entertaining others, she was reflecting back on the experience. She had heard the eruption rising from the grove below, the sound of animals perturbed by her vanishing act, she suspected. This only quickened her pace as she traveled incognito up the mountain path.

She ducked her head to avoid being nicked by the horns of two passing antelopes embroiled in an argument.

"Is it a long journey to get to the place we're going?"

"Long? No. Short? Yes—*if* we get tangled up inside of a web. Stuck within the woods. It could take forever."

"Stuck how?"

Buzz flew close to her face. "Spiders. Did I mention the spiders? Spinning their webs. Filled with tricks. They think they're so clever. Slinging silk out their ass. Making traps. But can they do this?"

Buzz scribbling the air in a light-show of motion, ending with his name spelled out. His name faded away.

"Impressive," said Kat, pausing to watch.

"They can't do that," said Buzz. "Only me. Others like me."

"Tell me about these woods."

"Not a problem. If you watch where you're going. And learn to weave and duck. You won't get stuck. It's tricky. Like I said. Sticky. The trick is not to panic. You start to run. You're done."

"Done?"

"Dead in your tracks. The more you twist and turn."

"Why are we going there… again?"

"We have to. To see the judge," said Buzz.

Kat was bumped by someone moving fast along the trail and in a reflex she blurted, "Sorry." She quickly covered her face.

"Watch yourself," said Buzz, glancing back. "Don't want to be seen. Once we get to the webbed woods you'll be okay."

"You just said it was dangerous."

"No danger of being followed. Not out of danger. No one goes into the woods unless they have to."

"That's not reassuring." Kat pulled her coat tighter. The night air was getting colder. The light was also dimming. Buzz was in a halo of mist. "What's happening?"

"Rises from the falls," said Buzz. "Condensates along this ridge. The mist. A sign we're getting close."

They had disappeared. Zhena was rubbing the orb with her arms to make the fog dissipate. She was casting a spell of makeshift expletives. Neither proved effective at returning visible clarification. In frustration she rose off her cushions flinging her many arms and spewing a tangle of silk graffiti against the wall. Her vitriol spent, she settled back down, waiting impatiently for better reception.

Kat was walking blind, guided solely by the firefly's yellow light. As the mist began to clear, Kat saw definitions of the ridge this path had taken them. On her left was the face of a cliff with nothing but sky dropping off on her right. She heard the roar of falling rivers echoing up from the valley below. As they rounded a bend Kat saw what looked to be a cave-like hole in the dark forest up ahead.

"We're here," said Buzz, zooming back then forward before he hovered back into Kat's face. "There. There it is! Right there!"

"You sound nervous."

"Me? Nervous? No. Why? Do I look nervous? I can do this. I can. I've done it before. Successfully."

As they reached the forest Kat saw a spiderweb veil spanning the branches like a white banner announcing the entrance to a nameless theme park ride. "You've never had a problem in there?"

"What?"

"A problem going through?"

"Who told you that? Was it Wyatt? Hazel?"

"No one."

"I'm still *alive*. And quick. Aren't I?"

To prove his vitality Buzz whirred in rapid circles around Kat as she flinched and swatted him away.

"Stop it," said Kat. She pulled back her hood to get a better look around, then peered into the forest's dark passageway. A noise from above startled her. She looked up to find Riley in a tree.

"What are you doing here?" she asked.

"What are *you* doing here?" Riley hopped down a branch.

"How did you find me?"

Hovering behind Kat, Buzz echoed, "How *did* you?"

"I find everyone." Riley hopped to a lower branch. "You do not want to go in there."

As the crow hopped to the ground Kat took a few more steps away down the path which led through trees shrouded in cobwebs. Buzz hovered back and forth to hurry her along.

"Move it—move it—move it," Buzz insisted.

"Come back," said Riley calmly.

"No," said Kat, moving away. "You were going to kill me."

Riley lifted his goggles to reveal his dark hooded eyes. His grin was even more disconcerting. "You're dead already. Halfway there. You will never make it out. Not through those woods. I will help get you to where you want to be. Come. Fly home with me."

"Stay away," said Kat.

"Go in there?" said Riley. "I would never dare."

"Good." Kat ran toward Buzz who glowed in the darkness.

"I said don't run!" shouted Buzz.

Kat slowed to a walk.

She was chilled by the crow's parting words as he flew off.

"I will see you on the other side."

Kat flinched as a cobweb brushed her cheek. She swatted away the sticky filaments. Buzz hovered a short distance in front of her, zigging and zagging, lighting the way.

"So far so good," he said. "Stay calm. Stay alert. Not to panic. No good to panic. Next part is tricky."

"Tricky how?"

The path came to an end, sharply turning. Kat caught up to Buzz who was waiting, hovering and looking down the path.

"See what I mean?"

Kat saw the shimmering webs. There were sheer walls formed of silk. The trail appeared to lose dimension. All she could discern was a hazy white darkness.

"It's a maze," said Buzz. "Amazing, right? These eight-armed bandits know how to mix it up and confuse you."

"Bandits?"

"They're a tricky sect. Never ever the same route. Ready?"

"After you," said Kat.

It was like a room full of mirrors, thought Kat, maneuvering around the almost opaque walls. Except there were no reflections, only dimensionless iridescence. She was beginning to lose her sense of balance and her bearings.

Buzz glanced back at her. "This is where I almost lost it last time. Be alert. Eyes ahead. Never look back."

"You just did," said Kat.

He glanced back again. "To warn *you*. How else—*whoops!* Steady. Not to panic. Don't panic! Okay—I'm panicking! *Help!*"

Buzz was embedded in a wall of silk, his wings stuttering.

"Stay still," said Kat. "You're making it worse."

His body was mummified in the web. Kat extracted the fibrous strands from his body.

"Help me. *Quick*. The last time this happened—"

"The last time!?"

"I don't know what happened. And I woke up elsewhere."

"You told me you had made it through!"

"Most of the time I do. No one's perfect. Hurry!"

"Hold still! Why do I need to hurry?"

"Did I mention the spiders? They're a fun bunch once you get to know them. So I'm told. I can't fathom them. Please, hurry."

"Almost done. There."

Once free, Buzz hovered close to express his exuberant gratitude.

In doing so he threw Kat off balance – toppling them backwards into a luxuriant quicksand of clinging silk. Kat twisted to free herself but only sunk them both deeper. She eventually stopped moving. Buzz was intertwined, face to face, his black eyes staring into hers.

"Sorry about that," he said.

"Now what?" said Kat.

"Pray."

Kat sensed peripheral movement of arms and legs before being engulfed and spun into a whirlpool of white.

When Kat awoke she was hanging upside down. Relatively sure of this, yet she was not certain. So tightly bound she felt numb. She was incapable of moving her arms, legs or head. Through the filmy gauze covering her eyes she could make out shapes and movement. She recognized one of the voices. The others were anonymous. Her diminished vision elevated her sense of hearing and she was able to determine, using echolocation, she was in a room, or maybe a cave. She could make out several mummified shapes hung, as she imagined herself to be, suspended from a ceiling. Motionless like stalactites. Her head felt heavy from a reflow of blood and the pull of gravity. The only movement and sound came from her pounding heart. She smelled fear and tasted it as she gulped for air.

Her sixth sense told her she was not a bat, more likely bait.

"Look what has *become* of you," said a voice from behind her.

"Why am I upside down? Who are you?"

"Have you forgotten me already?"

"I can't see you," said Kat.

"Use what abilities you still possess."

The white gauze covering her eyes reminded Kat of the interior walls of the fox's palace. She recalled the spider.

"In the lobby," said Kat. "You work for Scarlet. You're—"

"Zhena. I work for nobody. So good of you to drop in. Let me brush those cobwebs from your eyes. There. Is that better?"

Kat saw the multiple eyes. She began to tremble.

"It seems I have captured the prize. You are very popular."

"What are you going to do to me?"

"Beyond that which I have already done?"

"Are you going to eat me?"

Zhena laughed. "A tempting idea. You *would* be a delicacy."

"I'm just trying to find my way home."

"Aren't we all," said Zhena. "I envision you serving a purpose. I might keep you awhile."

A rainbow wavered before Kat's eyes as this creature flipped a scarf around her neck as she departed, wearing a diaphanous gown that was equally colorful. She turned her head to say, "Welcome, by the way. I do hope you enjoy your stay."

Kat watched, upside down, the behavior of Zhena, who left to inspect her captive guests hanging about. She had assistants, other spiders smaller than herself, who were dressed like attending nurses and consulting her as if she was the doctor in charge. They gathered around each entombed guest adding more layers of silk, smoothing and poking or prodding them with surgical instruments. Suspended by tenuous threads, each guest rotated from the slightest commotion caused by the attendants and their airstream of motion.

As these specimens spun, rotating languidly, twisting in the wind, Kat noticed the varying length or width of each one, concealed like larvae in a cocoon.

Zhena was back in her face again.

"Are you feeling rested?"

"Very," said Kat. "I would like very much to leave."

"What's the rush? You have yet to experience the full pleasures of my spa."

"This is a spa?"

"Where did you think you were?"

"I don't know," said Kat. "I don't recall how I got here."

"A common phenomenom. You do recall traveling with Buzz, your friend over there?"

Kat located a small bundle hanging from the ceiling across the room. His black eyes were rapidly blinking.

"What's wrong with him?"

"Nothing a little R & R can't cure," said Zhena. "Recognize anyone else?"

Kat was adjusting her mind to see this place as a resort where guests were vacationing. She noticed the protruding independently-rotating eyes peering out from one of the body wraps. "Is that Camille?"

"She is a friend of yours?" said Zhena. "Camille vacations with me often. She's a frequent flyer. One of my best clients."

"I was afraid," said Kat, "you were going to harm me."

"A widespread misconception. A spider, as I am too often called, is a maligned name. Many times I have heard others claim we look alike. That we are deadly. We bite. I suppose you too have heard these rumors? That we are nasty and cruel?"

"Well, yes, I guess I have," said Kat.

"You guess?" Zhena blinked her many eyes. "Let us be honest with each other. Shall we?"

Kat was distracted not only by her black opaque eyes but by her many arms doing multiple tasks. As Zhena talked she smoothed her scarf with one arm, admiring the craftsmanship of the binding silk with another, while she jotted notes on a clipboard with two more.

"I had no idea you were friendly," said Kat.

"And now you know," said Zhena, returning the clipboard to a holder attached to her upside-down guest.

"Why did you say you had captured the prize?"

"I meant it as a compliment. You are my honored guest."

"But why?"

Zhena snapped and gestured instructions to her assistants while her mesmerizing eyes kept their focus on Kat. "Call it a test. To see if your shape will hold. I portend you to be neither here nor there. You are at the end of your rope. Extraordinary. Yet expendable. Appreciate this moment as amendable."

"Amendable means a change for the better." Kat gulped, fearing the worst. "How is this better?"

Zhena plucked off a loose strand of silk. She idly wound it into a cat's cradle of elaborate patterns between her nimble fingers. "Fate is flexible. Like the countless coils of string at your disposal."

"What string?"

"The web within that spun you into *you*. Imagine these strings as spiral staircases you must climb." Zhena said this with a laugh as the strands of silk became a sticky cluster, which she flung into the trash. "Ah, but when they tangle, become a mess, reinvent yourself. I do admire your pluck for tempting death."

"When was this?"

"When you thought you were invulnerable, as children often do. Time now to close your eyes and rest instead."

The nurses were wheeling a cart with an apparatus containing cylinders and tubes toward Kat. "What's that?"

"Nothing for you to worry about," said Zhena.

"Is that a needle?"

"You will not feel a thing," said Zhena. "A little sting."

"Please don't," said Kat, attempting to squirm.

"You will feel at *home* in no time."

"Please let me go. Please. I *beg* you."

Kat began to cry, sobbing and choking with fear.

Zhena took a step back to observe, intrigued.

"You have defaulted to tears. *Begging* implies you are willing to make me an offer. Do you have something to offer?"

The gold bracelets rattled on her many wrists as Zhena brushed back hairs from around her mouth with her spiky fingers, giving the matter thought before signaling to her assistants.

"Cut the girl down."

Kat glimpsed the slash and arc of a machete, heard the snap of twine, and felt the sudden release and drop as she blacked out.

She awoke facing Zhena who was seated in a luxurious wicker chair surrounded by colorful pillows. Kat realized she was propped upright by a similar pile of cushions. She found it difficult to move her head. Her muscles were numb and tingling. Through an arched doorway she glimpsed the cavern of hanging bodies.

Kat examined the cozy parlor and the large intimidating spider. Sconces were flickering with lit candles. A table was between them. Upon it was a deck of cards.

"I am going to read your fortune," said Zhena.

"Why?"

"Why not?"

Kat had difficulty lifting her arms and legs. "What's wrong with my body?"

"Nothing. My medicine is wearing off." Zhena reached for the cards, shuffled them, fanning them with her four arms, before setting them in a stack on the table. "I normally have my clients cut them. But since you cannot."

Kat stared at the overturned card. It showed a colorful drawing of a star shining upon a nest of eggs supported by a branch above a field of shimmering water. White letters spelled out: "The Star."

Kat asked, "What does it mean?"

"Transcendence. Nature. Inspiration. Wonder."

"How does this relate to me?"

"Innocence. Let's move on."

Zhena overturned the next card.

Kat grimaced at the image of a tower on fire, collapsing while being struck by lightning. Ocean waves were crashing at its base.

"An unforseen catastrophe," said Zhena. "The Tower needs no

explanation. The vision speaks for itself.”

"That's bad, right?" asked Kat. "For me?"

Zhena four black eyes twinkled as she grinned. "A card no one wishes to receive. Yet enlightenment can follow danger and fear. There is always that."

Kat thought she recognized the next card. "A waterwheel?"

"Wheel of Fortune," Zhena stated. "Signifying a turn of events. Unpredictability. The need for purpose and control."

"Oh," said Kat, recalling what Izzy had told her. "I think I know the meaning. Discovering your abilities and how you fit in?"

"I am not sure you do." Zhena flipped over the next card.

"The Moon. I like the moon." Kat smiled hopefully.

"Who doesn't. It implies you are on a quest. To find meaning. As well you should. To unlock your—"

"Essence?"

"You interrupted me. *Again.*"

"Sorry." Kat managed to lift the weight of her arm to touch the necklace Hazel had given her. "I suppose I am on a quest. Trying to find my way home."

"Far too limiting. Search for the uncommon too." Zhena eyed the cystal acorn around Kat's neck before turning over the next card. "The Moon can bode unforseen perils. Which comes from tapping into its psychic powers. So be wary."

"All right," said Kat. "I will."

Zhena stifled a laugh.

"What? What is it?" Kat fingered her necklace.

"*Justice*," Zhena scoffed, then glared at her. "Stop fidgeting."

"That's a good card to get, right? Justice?"

"When the card is upside down it means *Injustice*. Lawlessness. A lack of balance requiring restoration. And... compensation."

"Which way is it turned?"

"That depends on your point of view."

"It looks right-side up to me."

"Which portends your disregard for authority."

"How? Why would you say that?"

Zhena stared back with her four unblinking eyes. "When you are not held accountable for your actions you become an outlaw. Are you an outlaw?"

"No."

"You are not escaping justice?"

Kat opened her mouth but said nothing.

Zhena gave a scornful laugh. "Ah, look. The King of Cups."

Kat said peevishly, "So what does he *portend?*"

"An open mind and open heart. Generosity. To a fault." Zhena brushed the card aside and selected the next. "Or the reverse."

"Selfishness, you mean. Well, *which* is it?"

"That will depend on you. Ah, The High Priestess. I believe you know her."

Kat looked at the woman's pretty face. "I do?"

"Feminine mystery." Zhena picked up the card to hold it closer to Kat's face. "You two have met?"

"I don't think we have."

"She represents passion. Also... fertility."

"What are you implying?" said Kat.

"The card clearly indicates you have been seduced."

"I have *not.*" Kat blushed.

"There are many kinds of seeds and means for dissemination. Unforseen as to whether they take root."

"Nothing like that happened."

"Do not play innocent. We are way past that card."

Zhena flipped over another.

"The Fool?" said Kat. "Is that supposed to be me?"

"If you need to ask... *well.*" Zhena glanced toward the arched passageway. "Look around. Many fools end up here. They follow their bliss. Foolishly taking risks on an adventure to chase a dream. To walk onto air off a cliff. Are you following my drift?"

"I guess," said Kat.

"However *grand* The Fool's aspirations and intentions may be, it helps to have a plan. Do you not agree?"

Kat wasn't sure how to answer. "Are there many cards left?"

"Interesting," said Zhena, revealing the next one.

"What does Judgement mean?"

"I was told you would pose a challenge to my intellect. You do not know the meaning of this word?"

"Of course I do!" The spider's tone angered Kat and emboldened her. "It depends on its usage. Wisdom and good sense are two of its definitions. Are you now going to tell me just the opposite?"

"If the card is reversed. A threat to your health and well-being. It could also mean a shift in consciousness towards understanding. On balance, you have made a decisive move. It may or may not lead you to your redemption and resurrection."

"Resurrection? What is that supposed to mean?"

"The next card provides a clue," said Zhena.

"Wonderful," said Kat. "The Hanged Man!?"

"How apropos. Relax, it is not all bad. You are among friends. Hung as they are. You have arrived. Present tense. Yes?"

"His face looks peaceful."

"The Hanged Man has attained spirituality. At the crossroads, where you find yourself now, self-sacrifice transcends social order. You see the world upended. That is how I prefer it."

"What are you telling me?"

"Everything." Zhena overturned a new card. "You are in limbo. The Hermit helps complete the puzzle."

"Why? Is he a good card?"

"He or she is neither good nor bad. A guide. See the lantern? He will counsel you. But beware. His isolation and retreat from the world can prove dangerous. His lessons are suspect. This recluse may prove to be either a prophet or a fraud."

"How do I tell which?"

The spider grinned. "How should I know? This is your journey. You must decide. I have my own problems. Last card."

Zhena turned it over. She positioned it above the others.

Kat's fingers touched her necklace. She was regaining feeling and control of her muscles, although her body tingled. Her other hand pointed to the card. "Above his head is the symbol for infinity."

"Clever you should notice. This card has potency."

"Why?"

"Observe the wand. The Magician oversees all the key elements in the deck. He is the sleight-of-hand artist. A shapeshifter."

Zhena was idly twirling a strand of silk around her finger. As if to demonstrate her own shapeshifting abilities, she produced more strands until there were several. The widening gyre of silk rose into the air like a rodeo rope trick, or an acrobatic balancing of spinning plates on long poles.

Kat watched mesmerized as the tornado of silk kept rising above her and spinning in the air. It dropped to lasso her body.

"Hey! What are you doing?"

Zhena yanked on the rope to tighten the coils. She then reached across the table to smooth with her many hands the silk fabric across Kat's chest, plucking off a few loose strands.

"I," said Zhena, "have decided to accept your offer."

"What offer?" said Kat.

"To release you. In return for what you will be giving me."

Kat struggled, unable to free herself.

"I'm afraid to ask what."

"You have no need to fear me," said Zhena.

"Caw-ha! How many lies is that?"

Kat recognized Riley's raucous laugh. She turned her head and was relieved to see a familiar face standing beneath the archway.

Zhena abruptly stood. "No one invited you! Get out!"

Riley spread open his black cape of wings to brush past Zhena's feckless assistants who were attempting to stop him. "Fear is good. Does no one ever listen to me?"

Kat looked up and smiled. "Are you here to rescue me?"

"I am not the hero type," said Riley, surveying the room and Kat bound in silk.

Zhena haughtily confronted Riley. Her four eyes aimed as if they were weapons that could fire laser beams.

He ignored her and glanced around, noting the overturned cards on the table. "Turning tricks and selling fortunes again? I see you've wasted no time relocating your den of iniquity, Madam."

"You have no right to criticize my business."

"It is my business to criticize."

"Get out!" shouted Zhena.

To rile her even more, Riley said, "Where is your hospitality?"

"You have no jurisdiction here!"

Kat was glancing back and forth at them squabbling when she heard a commotion behind her. Wyatt was clutching the doorway, fanning his face with his beret, busy catching his breath. His coat was covered with cobwebs. He gave her a belabored smile.

"I got waylaid…" He gulped for air. "By your host's gang of merry pranksters. They hassled me along the trail."

"While discovering those treasure troves?" said Kat.

Wyatt grinned as he entered. "Are you about ready to go?"

"Yes, please," said Kat.

"Get out! You too!" screamed Zhena, thrashing about, waving her arms and flinging silky spit against the walls and ceiling.

Kat was baffled by how powerless this spider suddenly appeared to behave when moments ago she had been so intimidating. Aside from the threats and spells cast on Riley and Wyatt, her wrath was aimed mainly on her furniture, breaking items to pieces and tossing them about as she stormed out of her parlor.

Both Wyatt and Riley tore off the sticky twine binding Kat to the chair, then lifted her up. She had trouble standing so Wyatt took her into his arms and carried her out.

"Are we leaving Buzz?" said Kat.

"He's here?" Wyatt surveyed the hanging bodies.

Kat pointed to a bundle with upside-down eyes frantically wide.

"We'll be taking him too," said Riley.

Zhena was now flanked by her entire staff. "Are you his spouse? Not a relative? Then *no!* You cannot have him! He is under my care. I will release him when he is cured and *ready* to leave!"

"You mean," said Wyatt, "after you've sucked him dry?"

"Excuse me?" Zhena showed her fangs as she smiled. "I do not *kill* my clients. That would be counter-productive. The only *potion* I inject them with is pleasure. So do not *insult* me. My exclusive resort provides unforgettable experiences shrouded in breathtaking views of floral gardens, tranquil baths—"

"Call it what you like," said Riley, "but I know better."

"I provide the most prestigious *spa* you will ever find. My guests feel comfortably numb here. Look how peacefully they hang. From my patented single-strung hammocks, now available for purchase online. I make each of my guests feel pampered and welcomed."

Riley sneered. "Except to leave. You don't make it easy."

"Everyone needs a vacation." Zhena snapped to be assisted by an assistant who handed her a packet. "What I offer is hard to resist. Here. My brochure. I will offer you a discount. Stay a spell."

Riley stepped forward. "Don't force me to call for backup. My lads like a good brawl. It's like a vacation. Relieves their stress."

Zhena waved her arms. "Who is this *fly* to you anyway?"

Kat told her, "Buzz was helping me to get—"

"*I* was helping you!" countered Zhena. She spat a wad of silk.

"Fine. Take the whiny little pest. His presence here is less fulfilling to me than an appetizer."

One of her arms swiftly snapped the dockline holding Buzz to the ceiling and tossed him at Riley. "Now get out!"

"Our gracious host says," mocked Riley, catching the bundle and nonchalantly exiting into the lobby with Buzz tucked under his wing like a football.

"I will be glad to be rid of you all! And that goes for you too, little girl! I wanted more out of you. A testimonial—at *least*."

Carried in Wyatt's arms, Kat asked, "What about Camille?"

"Out!" spat Zhena.

Wyatt tipped his hat, then left. "Camille will find her way back. We should leave now while Zhena is still in a good mood." He said this with a serious face before smiling, getting Kat to laugh.

Transported in Wyatt's arms, Kat had time to look around at the architecture and illustrated walls decorating the arched passageway. Chandeliers with flickering candles illuminated the hall. In alcoves there were statues spun from silk – an elk, two swans, four beetles. Between columns were murals. Mysterious panoramas of nature in its twilight moments.

"I never saw these," Kat remarked. "I was covered in silk."

Wyatt paused for Kat to look.

"These are stunning. So strange. Yet beautiful."

"Thank you."

Kat looked up at Wyatt's chagrined frog face.

He shrugged. "What can I say? I needed the work."

As they moved on Kat said, "Thanks for coming."

Wyatt narrowed his oblong eyes with a self-effacing look. "What are frogs for, if not for rescuing fair damsels in distress?"

Kat was compelled – though slightly repelled by his face – to give him a quick kiss on the lips, and did.

Wyatt stopped. "What possessed you to do that?"

"I was curious. To see if you might be a real prince."

"Sadly, no." Wyatt smiled back. "In another lifetime, perhaps. Do you think you can walk on your own?"

Kat nodded and Wyatt set her down. She held onto his jacket as they walked the remainder of the way through Zhena's elaborately furnished cave and out into the dark of night. Riley was brushing cobwebs off his cape of feathers. Buzz had cast off the mummy wrap and was busy testing his pilot light. It was the first time Kat had seen this firefly standing instead of hovering in the air. He was the size of a small child.

Riley came toward her. "Are you always this much trouble?"

Kat backed away. "Not always. No."

"Why can't you do as you are told? You keep resisting me!"

"Are you going to force me to go back?" said Kat.

"Not now! You can't." Riley pulled down his goggles to cover his eyes. "You broke the rules and that's that."

Wyatt countered, "If you want to return you can."

"Why? I get the feeling I'm not supposed to be here."

"How observant," stated Riley.

"Wait until things settles down," said Wyatt. "Everyone will be better prepared to accept you and welcome you back later."

"Later?" said Kat.

"Don't you want to go home?" said Buzz. "Isn't that the plan? The whole idea? The reason you ran? And why we got twisted and caught!? Trapped in a web! And I almost died!!"

"Calm down!" said Wyatt. "You survived. No one died."

"I *could* have," whined Buzz, slapping his abdomen. His yellow light continued to sputter off and on.

Kat looked up at the stars. They were shining in the sky like any other night. But how could they be the same stars? She recalled the vacations with her family, camping in the mountains, bundled in sleeping bags, her father calling out the names of constellations, her mother telling them all to make beautiful wishes. Kat's eyes began to mist as they left the sky, finding herself standing again beside a crow, a frog and a firefly. Buzz was looking over his winged torso at his abdomen which was now projecting a bright steady glow.

"It's your call," Wyatt told her, "as to which way we go."

Kat looked at the yellow path created by Buzz's glowing bottom and smiled. "Then, I guess… we follow the yellow brick road?"

Riley squawked. "Are you daft!? This road has no bricks!"

Wyatt expressed concern. "Do you need to rest?"

Kat shook her head. "No. I'm fine. Let's go."

Buzz lifted off to hover and flit, still in a snit. *"Phew!* Me too. Let's get off this mountain. I am down with that."

"No," said Kat. "I meant up!"

Buzz flew into her face. "Well which is it!? Make up your mind! Mine is made. I say down! You say up! Both ways get you home. But when the sun comes up – you're on your own!"

The firefly buzzed off, muttering as he flew up the path, glancing over his shoulder to say, "Yellow brick road—my *ass.*"

196

Angelo Iguana

Angelo Iguana was mindful of his existence balanced precariously at the edge of a cliff. Incrementally came the shift from darkness into lightness. The penetrating glimpse into deep space was erased by sunlight, returning to reveal the world as it was, a reflective bubble. The flat blackness of his surroundings took on shape. The arc of a horizon, the feathery edges of clouds, the outline of hills and treetops signaling the coming of dimension. Followed by the glorious color in which he flew.

The morning light awakened his senses in the purest sense. *This* was life, the essence of being alive. Wind coursing through his lungs. The cool morning breeze engulfing his skin as if to sculpt his body. Each sensation energizing his mind. His eyes opened wide to witness this nearby star coming into view as he rotated, perched upon a rock. Once again molecules were teased by the hint of light to reawaken and intermingle with excitement. He too felt a tingle of warmth.

Angelo was at peace, finally at one with the world. For too long he had felt stuck at two, at odds with nature, divisible. Yet being at odds meant he was mathematically closer to three. An odd number. Nevertheless, it felt strange, if not odd, being indivisible.

The instant he realized that he was, Angelo lost this singularity. His meditative state of oneness dispersed amoeba-like, reproducing him into a blob of twoness.

Numbers. Multiplicity. Molecules. Atoms.

Angelo scratched his nose and lifted his chin, cognizant of the splinters of pain in his limbs, but was posed to bask in the sun and rekindle his oneness. He equated this ignition to flying. His research had shifted from the physical into the metaphysical. If atoms could absorb energy from radiation, such as with light, in increments that launched electrons into the next permissible orbit – why not him? Angelo had come to believe his own mass of collective electrons was capable of making a similar quantum leap.

Flight. It was Angelo's primary dream. He watched and envied birds their ease of piloting the sky. He debated with his feathered friends over matters of evolution and quantum mechanics, which led on occasions to shouting matches about the uncertainty principle. Angelo was fairly certain it was not true. Certainly there had to be a unifying theory to explain all the madness around them.

Angelo saw the first spark of white blink on the horizon and he smiled. It felt like a warm kiss on the face. The perilous height from where he was positioned became evident with the advent of light. Certain death awaited anyone who fell off this rock.

Unless, Angelo grumbled, you were a *bird*.

Angelo rose, then fell, deciding to exercise his torn muscles by doing light push-ups at the cliff's edge. Let his feathered friends look down and laugh. He stood and approached the end, curling his long toes over the ledge, and imagined he was standing on a platform high over shimmering water, about to dive off. He gazed up to face down his fear. He spotted three hawks circling above, in a holding pattern, waiting for his next move. Despite the pain in his legs, he bent them in preparation to spring off, but stopped. He smiled at his audience before turning to hobble and limp across the desolate plateau.

Having regressed to twoness, he vented his grievances at nature by kicking at the tuffs of rugged growth along the way. By the time he arrived at his dwelling place he was repentant, finding renewed respect for these resilient plants that refused to die.

He entered his home, a vacuous structure carved into the cliffs by ageless wind and rain storms and other natural phenomenoms. The arching shelter resembled an airline hanger, at least in Angelo's mind. To others, it resembled an ancient monastery. It was his sanctuary, as well his workspace and research lab. Each one of his failed efforts at achieving flight – including the inevitable crashes – were littered about like broken trophies. He recovered the wreckage to be stacked there as visual incentives for him to keep going until he succeeded.

At the far end of this vaulted space he detected movement.

Angelo ducked behind the remnants of a dislodged tail assembly and splintered rudder.

"Hello?"

The voice echoed throughout the vast space.

Angelo shuttered his eyes to listen, then peeked above the rudder, squinting with his keen vision to combine all his senses.

"Is anyone here?"

There it was again! Angelo saw no one, only his contraptions in mid-assembly and the isolated piles of wreckage spread apart like sculptures exhibited in a museum. He mused in admiration at this impressive space. It *was* like an academy of science.

And yet he wondered. Having cloistered himself in this retreat, removed from society and living alone for so long, had he sacrificed his sanity.

Angelo decided he had nothing to fear but his own mind, so he made himself visible. He walked out into the open, craned his stiff neck, and asked, "Who is there?"

Kat emerged from behind a crumpled pile of metal. It had been a glider. Its once sleek frame now resembled a compressed arrow bent into an accordion shape, its nose stuck in the ground.

"Me."

"You," said Angelo.

"Oh," said Kat, "you're the one."

"The one what?"

"Who was taken away in the ambulance?"

"How did you get here?" Angelo gestured to a pair of cockpit seats placed in the dirt beside an airplane wing converted to a table. "I need to sit. Would you care to join me?"

As they took their respective seats, Kat surreptitiously perused his scaly blue-and-pink weathered face, the wrinkled lids of his eyes, neck waddle, then the spiny crest of feathery extensions trailing from the top of his balding head down his back. She averted her eyes from his striped and mottled severed tail.

He noticed her examination. "I'm regenerative. So…"

"Does it hurt?"

"What do you think?"

"How long does it take to grow back?"

"Did you come all this way to talk about my tail?"

"No." Kat reassessed her thoughts. "I was trying to make polite conversation. I thought if—"

Angelo was blunt. "What is it you want?"

Kat nervously rubbed her hands over her short dress, smoothing the hem against her harlequin tights, the motion shaking the beaded tassels of her skirt and leather jacket. She laughed unintentionally.

"What do you find so amusing?"

"Us," she said, fidgeting with the leather fringe, looking down then up into the dragon's intimidating eyes. "We're both…"

"What?"

"Colorful."

"Hum," he muttered, grumpy from the intermittent splinters of pain shooting up his spine from his tail and legs. "I don't know you. So I am therefore unwilling to venture an opinion on the extent of your *colorful* nature."

"I meant what I'm wearing," said Kat.

"Which is disposable. Interchangeable. Not really you."

"I suppose not. My name is Kat."

"Angelo," said Angelo. "Again, why are you here?"

"Wyatt, he told me—"

"Wyatt?"

"He's a frog. A painter, I mean. He found me—"

"He found you?"

"I was unconscious."

"And now you are awake?"

"I believe so."

Now Angelo was amused. He shifted in his pilot's seat to lift his amputated tail and elevate the stub onto a rock. "For us believing physicists, the distinction between past, present and future is only a stubborn illusion."

"Is that what you are, a physicist?"

"Those are not my words," said Angelo. "Though a sentiment I find applicable to our illusion regarding life and death. No, I am an inventor. An ex-judge. A philosopher. And a fool."

"Also a hermit?"

Angelo laughed. "Yes, I have become that too."

"I was told you could help me."

"So, you *are* on a pilgrimage?" Bemused, Angelo's eyes crinkled as he observed the rising sun, enjoying the mild breeze. He looked skyward and closed his eyes. "Did you come alone?"

"Yes," said Kat. "Not exactly."

Angelo opened one eye.

Kat explained, "I had help getting here. It was dark. A firefly offered to guide me. He lit the way."

"You came to see me in the middle of the night?"

"If we hadn't got trapped in a spiderweb I would have arrived sooner. I awoke hanging upside-down in a spa. At least that's what she told me it was. I'm not sure where I was."

"Zhena, she is up to her old tricks. How did you escape?"

"Wyatt, who I mentioned," said Kat. "And a crow, they—"

"Riley!?" Angelo sat up, adjusting his posture. "Was it?"

"Yes. Do you know him?"

"Who doesn't? He *mocks* me. He..."

Kat waited for the lizard to finish, but instead he stood. She saw him as a dragon again and sensed he might spew a fire-breathing remark that would be detrimental to her quest, so she quickly added, "He isn't here. I told him – both of them – I should come alone."

Angelo closed his mouth. "How did you decide that?"

"I'm not sure."

Across his lips slid a blue-forked tongue, followed by a smile.

"Wait here while I heat up some tea."

Kat stayed as she was told, waiting for his return. She watched him disappear behind the enormous clutter. Left with plenty of time to study her surroundings, Kat realized there was a theme to this mess. Each statuesque hunk of junk had been strategically placed, neatly consolidated into piles with ample space to walk around. Broken wings and wheels and propellers and props and instrument panels were fused together to form a statement. What that statement was, Kat wasn't sure.

Angelo emerged dragging his stubby tail across the rock floor. He carried a tray which held a steaming ceramic pot and two cups. He placed it on the airplane wing and poured the tea. With his long blue fingers cupped around one of the cups, he offered it to Kat.

"Thank you. Are you a pilot?"

"Whatever gave you that impression?"

He did not smile but his droll words made Kat grin. "All these plane parts piled about. A hunch, I guess?"

"Planes fly. These clearly do not."

"But they flew once?"

"Once. That is a key word. Briefly. A flight nonetheless."

"They all crashed?"

"Not much of a pilot, am I?"

"What do you do with them all?"

Angelo contemplated, sipping his tea. "I allow them to haunt me. Like remnants of a dream. Having them here has helped teach me. This is how I learn."

Kat was baited into asking, "What, exactly?"

"From my failures. From success we learn much less."

Silence prevailed. Kat was being encouraged not to speak, or so she sensed. They quietly sipped their tea in the morning sunlight. The beautiful new day was helping to calm her mind and get beyond her troubles and hectic emotions from the previous day.

"I have become Einstonian in my thinking," said Angelo.

"What does that mean?"

"The relationship among orbiting stones. Weights and measures, basically. A belief that reality is independent of how we observe it." He observed her confusion. He cradled his ceramic cup, green with a dappled glaze, similar to the one Kat held. He first blew on the hot tea before savoring each taste. "When events happen that cannot be explained, should they be dismissed as unreal?"

"I don't know."

"I do," said Angelo. "Which means, I do *not*. Phenomenons that we find inexplicable hold the missing key to what will unify the field theories of conflicting science. Existence is not random."

Kat silently sipped her tea.

"Or happenstance." Angelo's stare was penetrating and intense. "Take yourself. A fluke. No one knows why you are here. And yet, here you are."

"Here I am," echoed Kat with a smile.

"Why hold a grudge against the universe for not explaining the totality of its actions to us?"

"I don't... hold a grudge."

"It accomplishes nothing," Angelo added. "Like these *doubters* who mock religion – which is simply the architecture behind why we exist. Their denial is counterproductive. They deafen their minds to the music and beauty of the spheres!"

Kat sipped the warm beverage and smiled.

"It's tragic. You don't agree?"

"No—I mean, yes. I'm listening. It's interesting. I..."

Angelo tilted his head sideways, then up a notch.

"I have a confession to make."

"So confess."

She brought the cup of tea to her lap to hold it steady. "I was put on trial. In your village."

"I claim no rights of possession."

"You're missing the point," said Kat. "I was arrested and placed in a cage."

"By Riley, naturally."

"It wasn't fair how I was treated. They made fun of me in court. Nothing was taken seriously. I felt sure they were going to kill me. That's why I left and came here. To see if you could help."

Angelo chuckled. "Me? Help you? A runaway."

"I'm not a criminal."

"You broke the law by escaping justice."

"What justice? I did nothing wrong!"

Angelo held up an orange scaly hand to stop her. He examined his claws, scraping two long nails together, before telling her, "There are two types of instincts. One is to conserve and unify, the other to squander and destroy. The former is restraint, the latter erotic. An emotional release considered to be necessary, at times. Neither one is good nor evil. They are intertwined, either working in concert or locked in battle."

"Will you help me? I'm trying to find my way home. Wyatt told me you were a judge and—"

"Retired. I was unable to judge anymore. It was presumptuous of me to arbitrate on matters of right and wrong. Unbalanced as I had become myself. The scales of justice had tipped equally at both ends for me, spilling over. And weighing me down, to use a cliché, with guilt."

"Why? Criminals should be punished."

"I agree. But who are they?"

Kat said, "You know, the ones that do *bad* things. Kill?"

"No one does that here."

Kat gulped down the rest of her tea. "What do you mean?"

"The only bad things that ever happen here take place in the mind. A punitive damage more effective than anyone could imagine. As a judge, the most I ever accomplished was settling petty disputes. And my rulings – determining who was right, who was wrong, what was good or bad, like art – *subjective*. Inevitably it depends on one's point of view. And being the judge, my point of view ruled. These squabbles, given time, would have settled themselves. But acting as judge, who do you think accumulated the backlash of grievances?"

"This is very confusing," said Kat.

"As are words. Take words," said Angelo.

"Words?"

"Such as Dirt. The planet we reside on."

"Don't you mean Earth?"

"I meant what I said. Within our complex network called a solar system, we sometimes detect static-filled communications informing us of distant planets experiencing unrest. And if this turbulence goes unresolved it will destroy the alliance of neighboring planets. If not our entire galaxy."

"Are you serious?"

"Call it a metaphor." Angelo smiled. "A rumor. Pure analogy. We may or may not be in a precarious state. Even though we find ourselves seated upon a rock ledge."

"But we're not."

"We will be." Angelo rose. "Follow me."

"Do I have to?"

"Only if you want my help."

Kat rose to reluctantly follow this lizard. He stopped a few times to rummage though cupboards and chests, tossing miscellaneous items into a backpack. Without once looking back, assuming (or simply knowing) she would be there trailing behind him, he shuffled and softly whistled. She quickened her pace to move closer so she could hear the notes, but it was nothing she recognized. It was more like the repetitious warbling of a melodic bird.

Angelo stopped at the threshold of his dwelling, a nebulous line since this natural structure had no physical doors. The demarcation of interior and exterior was the smooth rock floor dropping off to the dirt. The depth no more than a street gutter.

"I want you to stand right here. Upon this precipice."

Kat stopped where she was told. "This is the ledge?"

"Can you balance on one leg?"

"Of course I can, if I had to."

Angelo patiently waited until she did. "Good. Keep that leg up. Now raise the other leg as well. Go on."

Kat questioned his nod of encouragement, his serious demeanor, before realizing he was joking. She laughed.

"I like your laugh," said Angelo. "Very colorful. Now…"

"Now what?"

"Hold your arms out on both sides and look down."

Kat accomplished the feat with ease.

"Do you fear losing your balance and falling off the ledge?"

"No."

"Set your foot down. Are you likely to fall off now?"

"Not at all," said Kat.

"You are balanced? In control of you faculties?"

"Yes."

"Good. I call this challenge the Precipitous Curb. It concludes our first lesson"

"What was I supposed to learn?"

"Mind over matter. Let us take a walk."

Kat kept up as Angelo sauntered, limping across the arid plateau. She had been wanting to get up the courage to ask, and finally did. "You're an iguana, right?"

"Would it matter if I was a fish?"

"Maybe. I guess not."

"Or a snail?"

"I was only curious."

"I had been informed you are part feline."

"Who told you that?"

"A little bird."

Kat finally realized where Angelo was taking her. Onto a large rock that extended like a gangplank into air. She stopped.

"Where are we going?"

"Out there," said Angelo, pointing to the sky.

"There's nothing there."

"There is more *there* than here. Come."

Angelo walked to the end of the rock and set down his backpack, waiting for Kat to arrive. She took baby steps toward the edge.

"This is a scary place."

"Place is a state of mind. Where we reside at a given moment is not exclusively external. Words create reality too. Pleasure. Pain. Euphoria. Heartbreak. Optimism. Fear. Rapture. Metamorphosis. A Quantum Leap. These are all places. Transitional states of mind. There is no certainty where we will be next. Each moment is now. Reality amounts to flickering lapses in time, as infinite layers of *now*. And with this constant motion we think of ourselves as being at rest. When in actuality we are zooming through space. Have you sensed this feeling before?"

Being so close to the cliff's edge caused Kat to shake nervously. She recalled the sensation she had felt at the entrance to Evolsdog with the simultaneous rising mist and falling rivers.

"Upon the bridge."

"At Zufall?"

"Yes," said Kat. "The waterfall."

"No. *Zufall* is the embodiment of chance and probability."

Kat furrowed her brow. "You mean, us being here now?"

Angelo shook his head. "No. Our being here is not by chance. Your path is predictable. Calculable. Causality times the curvature of space divided by quantum mechanics equals probability. That is where you will find yourself. Always. Confused?"

Kat bobbed her head.

Angelo nodded back. "Uncertainty. We are collective bodies of moving particles held together by thought. A quantum leap is the energy it takes to move us to a new level. Our existence is perfectly irrational. Logically we should not exist."

"But we do," said Kat.

Angelo shrugged, stretching his muscles.

"Why?"

"Faith trumps logic. Are you ready?"

"Ready for what?"

"For lesson number two. Move all the way to the rock's ledge and stand as you had before, with both feet planted solid."

"Why?"

"I will show you why."

Kat inched forward to stand beside him. The depth of space to the valley and river far below made her unsteady. "I'm scared."

"Of falling?"

"Yes."

"Of losing your balance? Losing control?"

"Yes."

"Nothing has changed." Angelo spit. The plume of liquid arced and fell straight down. "Except the stakes. Much higher. Our lives are literally on the line. Yet there is no wind to hamper our ability to stay balanced, only fear to overtake the mind."

Kat began to wobble. Angelo noticed and took hold of her arm and pulled her back from the ledge. "End of lesson two."

"Dare I ask what lesson *three* will be?"

"To fly."

"Fly?" Kat stepped back further. "Are you crazy!? No—don't bother answering." She turned and walked away. "I'm leaving. I've had enough. All your mumbo-jumbo—"

"*Wait*," said Angelo.

Kat stopped and turned. "Give me a good reason."

"I am going to teach you how to get home."

"Falling to my death? No thank you."

"Flying. You will *not* die."

"I don't have wings. I'm not a bird."

"Nor am I. Regrettably. But we can still fly."

"Right. Is that how you lost your tail?"

Angelo brushed his failures aside with a smile, bent down and unzipped the backpack, dumping two smaller packs onto the rock.

"What are those?"

"Parachutes. Which we will *not* need. A backup plan only to reassure you. To ease any fears you might have."

"I have plenty," said Kat. "I suppose the rumors are true."

"What have you heard?"

"That you *lost* your mind," Kat blurted.

Angelo calmly grinned. "I found it."

Kat wasn't so sure. She recalled the image of The Hermit card. The spider had forewarned her about this recluse who was either a fraud or a prophet. "Then why leave? Give up everything? And what's wrong with having mirrors!?"

Expecting this lizard to lash back, Kat had tensed. But Angelo passively settled his body down upon the rock.

"You shouldn't believe everything you hear."

With noticeable discomfort, he shifted his torso into an upright position, crossed his thick legs, tucked aside his stubby tail, before lifting his chin.

"I will show you what you want to know. Come sit."

"I don't think so." Kat turned to leave.

"What I am *proposing* is not what you think."

Kat stopped, her curiosity piqued. "How do you mean?"

"Metaphysical flight." Angelo comically pinged the side of his head with an extended forefinger and sharp nail to mimic a gun. "I have stopped putting my life and limbs at risk. Come back."

Kat didn't budge. "How is what you're telling me possible?"

"The same way we are possible. Sit with me."

Angelo patted a spot on the rock beside him and rearranged the parachute packs, preparing for an impromptu picnic as he lay down a red and white checkered cloth, then removed from the backpack a thermos and two cups.

Mentally sorting through her minimal options, Kat meandered back and stood, hesitating to sit. "Convince me."

"Tea?"

"How long has it been in there?"

"Not long. I had an inkling of a premonition you were coming. Do you prefer your tea hot or cold?"

"What you gave me before was good. Hot, I guess."

Angelo held up the metal thermos and shot fire from his mouth for a few seconds. "That should do it. Join me. Please."

Kat was stunned, realizing he *was* some kind of dragon.

"You didn't see that." Angelo winked and pointed again with a handgun to his head. "Intuition is quicker than the senses."

"I hope I don't regret this." Kat sat down.

"Oh, you will. Many of our actions are regrettable. No, I take that back. You will *not* regret this journey. Sugar?"

"What? No, thank you."

"Good. I forgot the lumps. It does make the flight sweeter."

"How is this supposed to work?"

"Accept," said Angelo, pouring the tea. "And it will."

"I'm not sure I can... *accept*... whatever."

"Accept the beauty of this unfolding day. Breathe. Relax."

"Is there a chance I will die?"

"Cookie?" Angelo opened a tin of wafers.

Their unexpected appearance was distracting. Kat took one.

Angelo dipped a wafer in his tea. He nibbled off a corner then sipped from his cup. "There is always that chance."

"I don't want to die. I like being who I am."

"Yet you want to leave this place."

"Only to go home. I want to remain alive."

"Are you?"

"Am I what?"

"Truly alive."

"You're scaring me."

Angelo nodded sagaciously. "Yes, each time we close our eyes to sleep and dream we risk never waking. You will find your way home once you believe you will fly and not die. Awakening is the essence of who we are."

Kat ate the small cookie in two bites, realized she was hungry, and reached to take another. "May I?"

"If you must," he said with a tone of mischief. "I insist."

Kat set her cup on the rock. As she ate, she reached up to touch her necklace. She felt nothing there. "It's gone!"

Puzzled by her outburst, Angelo asked, "Your fear is gone?"

"No! My necklace! I just had it! It was... *stolen.*"

Kat knew when it had happened. The spider had plucked it off her like a loose strand of silk. Her eyes began to well with tears.

"Why does it matter? Exhale. Breathe in this lovely—"

"Shut up! I was told it was a key to finding my way home."

"By whom? Who would tell you such a thing?"

"A squirrel. Hazel."

"She is charming. But also *nuts.*"

"Also Camille, she—"

"A chameleon?" Angelo chuckled. "Quite colorful, these lizards, yet fickle." He winked before sipping his tea. "Tell me what this necklace meant to you. No, more importantly, what it looked like."

"It was shaped like a nut."

"Naturally."

"A crystal acorn. It had a gold cube in its center."

Angelo pointed to her cup. "Your tea is getting cold. Drink up. Relax. And breathe. I know this nut. The meaning is clear to me."

Kat finished her cookie and sipped her tea. "Clear? How?"

"A praying mantis lives there. Inside the gold cube."

"That's impossible," said Kat.

Angelo chuckled, licking tea and crumbs off his lips. "Not *inside* the crystal. In the gold house at the top of this mountain. He is who you will most definitely want to visit after me."

"Then what am I doing here?"

"Having tea. And learning to fly."

"I think I'll skip lesson three and walk there instead."

"No one arrives there by walking. All paths lead into thorns. Overgrown with nasty stuff along the way. He prefers the solitude. Stay. Finish your tea. You have to *fly* in. Unannounced."

"Will he mind?"

"Of course he will! Wouldn't you?"

"I don't want to barge in and upset him."

"Be charming. He will be less likely to bite your head off."

"He might bite my head off?"

"He has been known to do such things. It is rumored. Relax. Breathe. First sit and savor the moment that is now."

"I'm feeling a little sick to my stomach."

"That will pass. As all things do."

"Did you put something strange in this tea?"

"Anxiety," said Angelo. "That is what you are feeling and what has upset your emotions. Nothing but herbs. Relax. Breathe."

"Stop saying that. It's not helping me."

"Because you are not listening. Here, put this on. Like so."

Kat took the satchel. She watched this old man – lizard, iguana, dragon – strap the other parachute around his shoulders and arms. She did the same then found the belt that snapped and synched the pack snuggly to her back. She touched the loose cord at its side.

"*Stop,*" Angelo told her.

"I wasn't going to pull it." said Kat. "It's the ripcord, right?"

"Only at red. Then you panic. And pull. You are nowhere near there, yet. You are in the yellow zone. *Anxious.*"

Angelo grinned placidly, amused at her chagrin.

Kat grimaced. "Ha-ha. Now what?"

"Close your eyes and take in a long deep breath."

"Why? What is that supposed to do?"

"Keep you alive. Oxygen, remember?"

Kat squinted, finally shutting her eyes, breathing deep.

"Again," said Angelo, closing his own lids. "Again. And again. You will begin to see a white light glowing around your body."

"What if I don't? Shouldn't we be standing or—"

"No more talking. Listen. And *breathe*. Take a deep breath. Allow this light to flow around and comfort you like a warm robe. As you continue to breathe and exhale, visualize yourself lifting off and out of your physical self. The darkness you see is beginning to lift too. Visualize shapes taking form. Into a vague horizon. A hazy shade of dawn. A blur of colors gradually sharpening to become a deep valley between mountain walls. Feel yourself moving through this space. Slowly, before gaining speed."

Kat saw nothing and felt foolish. The sparkling static started to move, like dots hinting at connections, reassembling into glimpses. Familiar shapes took subtle form inside the dark space of her mind. She felt for a second she should clutch her backpack, something firm, but soon forgot she was solid, an object of weight, and she began to float. A flutter of panic passed through her heart and lungs until she remembered Angelo's instructions to breathe and exhale. Just as her heart slowed – she felt herself accelerate.

She was zooming high over water. Over a magnificent mirror sparkling in her mind's eyes. The sky rippling within its surface like an undulating gateway reflecting a world of hidden truths.

She heard Angelo's voice from somewhere near, "You can move wherever you want. Think where you want to be and go."

Moving erratically fast and slow, Kat saw the lake's shoreline miles away, saw the patch of greenery, thought to be there – and was. Startled by how fast she arrived, she had to think fast to veer up and over the treetops before smashing into them.

She heard Angelo's laughter far off.

It was like operating a new devise – which was herself – but not familiar with the controls. She drifted upwards in a gentle arc and began floating, in idle mode, with her arms extended, remaining still. While slowly rotating, she saw a sparkle of gold on a mountaintop, which came and went. Twisting her body to reverse her course, she spun out of control and fell in a vertical drop, helplessly flailing her limbs to recover before she was caught. Missing the lake by inches – swept up within a moving shadow. A spray of cold water stung her face as she was launched back into the sky.

Chilled, yet refreshed, she heard a caw and glimpsed the wings of a departing bird. She was questioning her senses as she drifted for a moment warming in the sun. Her heartbeat had slowed, echoed in her motion as she floated in the blue pool of a warm sky. Calmly she turned and saw once again the gold structure on the mountaintop. Aiming her mind and sight on this destination – she flew at lightning speed toward it – then let out a yelp as the rock ledge neared – not knowing how to brake or stop!

Kat opened her eyes, her heart beating fast, setting both hands flat against rock. Angelo was seated facing her and smiling.

"What happened?" said Kat.

"You know what happened. You flew."

Kat observed the precipice they were on. Closely resembling the one they had been on. But the tea, blanket and backpack were gone. She looked behind her and saw off in the distance a gold windowless building. It was nestled within a bramble of flowering bushes.

"This isn't possible," said Kat.

"You may be right. But wrong not to try. Start by doing what is necessary, then what is possible, and suddenly you are doing the impossible. Those are not my words."

Angelo's orange snakeskin arm reached toward Kat, too stunned to react or move – or ask what his intentions were. His long sharp fingers clutched her ripcord and pulled. Releasing her parachute to drop from its pack with a soft rustle.

"End of lesson three."

chapter twelve

Prater Mantis

Prater Mantis, in solemn prayer, had his multiplex eyes dimmed, his spiked translucent forearms bent at the wrists, clutching a precious relic. Every so often he peeked at the albino face, puzzled by this creature in the oval pool. Angled this way or that, no matter how he turned its handle, the trapped liquid remained perfectly flat. His reflection was perplexing.

He set the object face down on his bed of rose petals and rose to stroll in crazy-eight circles around the walls of his shrine. The vast cubicle had no windows to distract him. Instead, the interior space was awash with off-white ethereal murals, designed for him to blend into his surroundings, to help merge his mind with the hint of clouds and foliage and colors that he now and then would detect. On rare occasions he would stroll the exterior grounds. The garden seemed to attend to itself. The roses were in constant bloom.

Having no windows was comforting to Prater. No eavesdropper or shutterbug could ever be found listening in or peering through the looking glass. There was no transparency. Once upon a time he had lived in a glass house. But never again. His privacy was now in tact. Secure in his seclusion. All the light and air he required was filtered down a hexagonal stairwell, a geometrically-domed ceiling opened at its center. Rain found its way in too, to trickle down the escher architecture designed to meticulously drip from cleverly-concealed gutters into his multitude of plants.

A sustainable existence. His happiness contained. His spirit free to meander wherever it chose.

His imagination ran wild – fabricating puzzles so elaborate few minds ever solved them. It hardly mattered. So intricate in design, they stood alone as art. On display in museums, boutiques and toy shops throughout the village. These puzzles took many forms. As word games, drawings, sculptures. Tricks of perspective were his trademark. Especially with the seemingly solid objects that opened.

When unlocked, if ever, the hidden contents boggled the soul with pleasure.

He had three newfangled puzzles ready for departure, all aligned and wrapped for pickup upon a unique shelf that resembled the last step upon a rung of stairs. This staircase ascended in irregular back-and-forth perspective until it diminished and disappeared high upon the wall. Basically going nowhere.

He paced, waiting for the pigeon carriers to arrive, rubbing his hands for warmth (he told himself) even though all the rooms in his domain were self-regulated and cozy at all hours. Deciding to step outside and search the sky, he grabbed a white robe off a hook and began to venture down the corridor constructed in a zigzag maze to a triangular entryway which had an open-vented door.

Meanwhile, Kat was crawling through the barbed mesh of rose bushes that encompassed this golden cube. She could see it up ahead towering above this unkept garden, yet the closer she got the further away it seemed to be, painfully out of reach. She was snagged again by thorns and cried out. Stopping to suck blood from her finger, she carefully assessed her location in this dense thicket and felt trapped. So tired, she wanted to sit down or simply collapse, but she pushed on. The bushes were so tall she decided to get down on her stomach and crawl like a snake. She wove through the gaps at the base.

The withered branches and dead thorns continued to prick her but she was making better progress. Breathing dust and sneezing, she emerged from the thicket. She stood, brushing herself off as best she could. Her harlequin tights were ripped, her green dress torn, leather jacket sliced, her exposed skin scratched and bleeding.

"Why am I doing this?"

She had begun talking to herself. Her mind was still troubled by the iguana or dragon or whatever he was who had suddenly become an old man. And had given her a benevolent smile before he turned and jumped off the rock precipice.

Alarmed, Kat had gone to the ledge and found only birds gliding in the sky, before spotting the receding white puff of silk drifting to the valley floor and river below.

As she tore off pieces of her tights she began questioning whether she should have jumped too. She used the cloth to dab at the spots of blood on her legs and arms. "Why did I even come here? God— look at me!"

"I am looking," said Riley.

Startled, Kat found the crow perched on a monolithic rock. It resembled an unmarked grave.

"How did you get here!?" she asked.

"Now *that*," he told her, "is a silly question."

"I meant, *why* are you here?"

"As your friend," said Riley. "Pay attention."

This prompted Kat to view the grounds. She was standing on a moat of pebbles which encompassed the gold structure. There were many more rock markers, tall and short, individually placed, others arranged in clusters, all jutting from this lake of granules which was raked in circular and serpentine patterns. A barren landscape that sharply contrasted the surrounding wall of thorns and bright color. The rose blossoms provided an enclosure of sweet fragrance.

Riley asked her, "How did *you* get here?"

"You wouldn't believe me if I told you," said Kat.

"I believe you crawled."

"Through thorns." Kat stopped to wipe her forehead and saw blood smeared within the dusty sweat. "No worse than what you put me through back there."

"That? It was all a farce."

"A farce!?"

"A mockery. An initiation. A sham. A foolish play. You would have realized that had you stayed. But no."

Kat cocked her head. "What do you mean, no?"

"You chose to go."

"What'd you expect? I wasn't about to stay and die."

"*That* was the point. To make you aware."

"Aware of what?"

"That you had a choice."

"Wait. What would have happened if—"

"I cannot say," said Riley. "That will be for another day. Buzz sends his apologies, by the way. For the way he behaved. He had a nervous breakdown, he claims. He is fine now, it is safe to say."

"Why are you talking in rhyme?"

"Am I?"

Kat shook her head. "I'm glad he's feeling better."

Riley watched her attempt to clean herself and decided to preen himself too. "Your efforts to get back to where you once were and overcome the odds is admirable. I wish for you a safe trip."

The remark got Kat to blurt, "Thanks. I *did* almost die getting here. Wherever I am. I can't explain how, but I was flying. I lost control and—"

"I know. I was there."

Kat questioned his sincerity with a frown.

"Lucky you are a *cat*. Nine lives? I have lost track."

Kat grimaced and looked around, focusing on the gold structure, symmetrical on all sides. Its top was a triangular zigzagging parapet that led to an observation point. She found it puzzling there were no windows. Along the base she noticed a triangular opening.

"What happens next?"

"That depends on you," said Riley.

"I guess I should go inside then?"

"I would not. But I am not you, as you have said."

"That's not being very helpful," said Kat.

Riley fluffed out his winged cape as if preparing to exit from a stage. He gave her a dramatic bow. "It was nice knowing you."

"Will I ever see you again?" From the pebbles Kat stepped onto a flat stone. Another was nearby. She hopped onto it.

"Wyatt believes so. He asked me to say goodbye."

Kat hopped to another rock, then another. "Goodbye, I guess. I don't really know what to expect."

She looked back but Riley had already flown off.

"I guess no one ever does," she said to herself. She was getting closer to the triangular opening. "Now I'm talking to myself again. This can't be any good. I suppose it's possible no one is home."

As she neared, she realized the opening was smaller than she first perceived. She looked around before deciding to get on her knees. With a last look up and a quick prayer to God, whom she wondered might be there, she ducked and told herself as she crawled inside, "Here goes nothing."

And nothing is what she saw when she reopened her eyes.

Complete darkness.

"I am not liking this at all," she murmured.

She continued to crawl, feeling around. She felt the walls and realized they were arched and getting taller and wider the further in she went. She thought she might be able to stand without hitting her head and did, grazing it slightly. She was mildly comforted by the smooth and warm surfaces of both floor and walls. With her arms extended she could touch both sides, but the passageway gradually began to expand, getting too wide to hold on.

"Hello?" she called out softly.

Up ahead she saw something white. Her eyes, she rationalized, were adjusting to the lack of light. Whatever it was she saw was not moving and blocked her way. Her fingers proceeded to glide along one wall, keeping her balanced. Suddenly the white object moved.

"Who invited you?"

"Oh," said Kat, stopping. "You're alive."

"What *are* you?"

The voice was soft and calm yet stern. Kat could see, barely, the formation in the shape of a triangular head.

"You must be the praying mantis?"

"You must be an intruder."

Kat heard a flickering sound and saw its antennae and long arms raised, bent at the wrists. "No! I mean, I didn't mean to intrude."

"What do you call *this*? You have entered my home—"

"I'm sorry—"

"Unannounced and *un–in–vit–ed*."

Kat rapidly explained, "I was told I should come here."

"Who would tell you such a thing?"

"An old man—lizard. Iguana, maybe. Also a spider. She—"

"You seem confused."

"I am. Very. May I come in?"

There was a long silence. "Did you see any pigeons?"

"Excuse me?" said Kat.

"Outside."

"No. Only a crow."

"Riley?"

"Yes, he also said—"

"Please be quiet. You may follow me."

Kat did as she was told. She followed this hunched figure who shuffled down the dark corridor. She kept her mouth shut but was eager to ask a flood of questions that were queuing up in her mind, waiting for the opportune time to speak. The passageway zigged and zagged and she glanced at the artwork hung on the walls as light incrementally overtook the darkness. She was tempted to stop and stare – make a comment – so compelling were the drawings. The art showed perspectives of vistas more puzzling than complete. She bit down on her lip to keep her mouth from talking.

They were approaching a square opening that revealed a room glowing uniformly with a gentle light. She was surprised as her host abruptly pivoted to stop her from going any further.

"Let me look at you."

Kat felt embarrassed. This tall creature with its triangular head was wearing an immaculate white robe. It covered his narrow frame but exposed his boney neck, wrists and hands. She averted her eyes from his ghoulish head. She noticed his spindly ankles and feet and looked away again. The floor formed a pattern of squares, white and grey marble, polished to a high sheen. And very clean. Which made Kat all the more uncomfortable – aware of how dirty she must have appeared in the light.

"I can explain," she said.

"Silence. I prefer it. Allow me to observe."

Prater did, looking her up and down, turning her around with the tips of his long slender fingers, pushing her, pulling her back.

"You must undress."

"What?"

"You are a mess."

"I know but—"

"*What* did I tell you? Before?"

"To be silent?"

"Look to your left. There are robes. Choose one. Discard what you came with and deposit the filth in here." He indicated a slot in the wall then pushed at a section of the wall. A door swiveled open. "That means everything. You will locate a mechanism intuitive to use which will provide a waterfall of warm water. Wash. Then dry. *Then* you will be allowed inside, where you will find me."

With that, Prater left her. Kat still had her mouth open. She shut it, but continued to stare into the glowing space. She watched the praying mantis walk around a minimalistic sofa, maneuver past a bookshelf, then disappear. Kat backed away into the corridor. She leaned against the wall, slipped off her tattered ballet shoes, pulled off her jacket, then her torn dress and ripped tights, dropping them in a pile on floor. Scooping up her clothes, she pushed them through the wall. She then grabbed a robe off its hook. All the robes were white and identical.

Prater Mantis was seated in a lounge chair when Kat emerged some time later feeling clean and refreshed, hair dry, shaken loose. Walking barefoot she was draped in the soft luxurious robe cinched at her waist. The length of the robe was longer than she was tall and so it trailed behind her as if she had a tail. She expected the floor to be cold but the marble was pleasingly warm.

She opened her mouth to speak but saw his rigid expression.

"Radiant heat," he told her.

"Ah," Kat murmured, nodding. She smiled and sat, reclining in a chair similar to the one her host was ensconced in, his long limbs crossed over his chest, appearing to be relaxed. His narrow, almost skeletal body made her ill at ease. She shivered, averting her eyes from his triangular head and eyes bulging at both ends along the top. His albino translucent skin eerily matched the body images stored in her mind of aliens from outer space. His curving antennae vibrated minutely. His pinched mouth sported whiskers.

"Relax," he told her. "I will not bite your head off."

"Thank you. Thank you for the robe."

"It is for me more than for you. Your body is strange. The robes suit us better. You have something you wanted to say?"

Kat had. Now she was unable to assemble a coherent thought or sentence, or recall the queue of questions she had misplaced.

"Good," he said, leaning back. "Those who are overly talkative have the least to say."

Kat mutely scooted back against the recliner, making an effort at relaxing, crossing her legs at the ankles, lacing her fingers together. They were in the center of the room. She looked around curiously, avoiding the direct stare of the praying mantis. The geometric use of light and shadow shaped the interior space in a most puzzling way.

At one moment she thought she was looking at a pattern of lizards before they tranformed into a flock of intertwined birds, then into a school of fish. An alignment of cubes and spheres upon another wall seemed to diminish then expand, creating an illusion of movement within an infinite space. She looked upwards and became lost in the receding rectangular dome of light.

She was deciding what she should say, trying to select her words carefully before addressing this creature.

"Is there anything I can get you?" asked Prater.

Looking back and forth between his two milky eyes, Kat saw the black dot in each one move, dilating and contracting, in response to changes in her expression and composure.

"Answers," she said.

"Ask me anything you like."

"Who are you?"

The praying mantis thinly smiled. "I am known by many names. The professor, by some. My name is Prater."

"Prater? But that means..." Kat stopped herself.

Her host tipped his head as an indication for her to continue.

 "Prater means... well, empty chatter and foolish talk."

"Amusing, isn't it? A name equated with endless babble."

"You're also a praying mantis?"

"That is my current situation, yes. I too enjoy a good laugh."

"Can you get me home?"

"Describe this place."

"Home is where I was before today, and yesterday. Living with my parents. In a house with my brother and sister too. Not that we always get along – perfectly. Nothing is perfect, I guess."

Kat sensed this creature was getting impatient.

"But we care about each other. I mean, it's complicated. We're different, each of us, but alike. Not—"

"Like me?"

"We're human. That's all. Yes."

"Why do you wish to return to this imperfect place?"

"We love each other. I miss them. And my life before... this."

"What is the last thing you remember?"

"From when?"

"Before you arrived here."

"I'm not sure," said Kat.

"Think. Close your eyes. You *do* know how that is done?"

Kat had begun to close her eyes but opened them. "Yes. I know how to close my eyes and *think*."

Prater prodded with his pointy chin. "Well?"

Kat closed her eyes.

"Tell me the first vision you see."

She tried but saw only darkness. Not a single image emerged. She began to fret, feeling lost, wondering if anything was there to be found. Then she glimpsed a nest. Blue eggs inside it. Within reach. She was balanced on a branch, about to reposition the nest that had been disturbed, on the verge of falling. When suddenly the world broke apart.

Kat opened her eyes. The praying mantis was holding an oval object by its handle and languidly fanning himself.

"There was an earthquake. I think."

"You think?"

"That's what I said. I think because I can't remember anything after that."

"Puzzling." Prater raised his chin. "Anything else?"

"Not since I woke up here. Not here, *here*, but in a meadow. And a frog was standing over me."

"And this frog, does he or she have a name?"

"Wyatt."

"Ah, as I figured. He painted my murals."

Kat glanced at the diaphanous murals encompassing them, saw

the ghostlike vistas of nature. "This is so strange."

"What is it you find strange?"

"The coincidence. Wyatt. That—"

"More than one event, by chance, is occurring simultaneously?"

"Yes."

"No," said Prater. "Nothing here happens by chance."

"Then…" Kat scanned the room again, examining the interior. With both of them robed, reclined in chairs, facing each other under a gentle shower of light, the temperature clement, the room peaceful, Kat felt as if she was at a resort. Recuperating at an exclusive spa. It was nothing like the spider's den. She heard no external noises or internal humming of electrical devices. Only a peaceful silence that lulled her mind. Physically exhausted from her efforts to get there, she was surrendering to the tranquil comfort. The balm so soothing she no longer was bothered by the scratches on her arms and legs.

Kat asked, "Can you help me get home?"

"You never left."

The pendulous motion of his fan distracted her.

Prater added, "You were transformed."

"What do you mean?"

"Metamorphosis." The praying mantis extended his long arm toward Kat as he told her, "You can be anything you want to be as long as you know who you are. Paradoxically, once you realize this, you begin to lose your sense of self. Here."

Prater was offering her the object he had been using as a fan.

"Look. If you must."

She glimpsed the walls reflected in the frame of glass as she took hold of its handle.

"It's a mirror."

"An item not generally allowed here," said Prater.

"Why not?"

"These frozen pools distort reality. They expose hidden truths.

Dangerous when viewed."

Kat hesitated, but began to lift the mirror.

"You may not like what you see."

She saw striped fur, pointed ears, green eyes, oval pupils, black nose and whiskers. Shocked, she watched the face of this cat open its mouth and widen its eyes.

"How did this happen?"

"You're awake."

The voice now sounded feminine.

She looked over the mirror to question this praying mantis but saw herself. She was standing at the foot of the bed. A little girl. Who moved toward her. She was wearing a red dress similar to the one she was wearing when she fell from the sky. How could this be? Equally disconcerting was the skin of her hand that held the mirror. It was parchment thin, wrinkled and aged. She hesitated, yet was compelled to look back into the mirror – and was startled again by what she saw.

"I'm a woman," said Kat. "How did I get to be so old?"

She dropped the mirror to her chest. She was lying in a bed, she realized. She looked at the little girl staring back at her.

"Who *are* you?"

"It's me. Kitty."

The little girl stepped closer.

"Kitty?"

"Yes, Grandma."

"I thought..." Kat shook her head. "You were me."

The girl giggled. "I was named after you."

Confused, Kat looked around to assess the room. The walls had changed. The geometric patterns were gone. Wherever she was felt unfamiliar, yet she recognized she was inside a bedroom. Beneath the covers of a queen-size bed, dressed in a nightgown, her body was at rest, inclined and propped up by several pillows.

"Where did the praying mantis go?"

Kitty's smile widened. "Do you mean Prater Mantis?"

Kat frowned. "Do you know him?"

"Of course I do, Grandma. You told me all about him."

"I did?"

"Everyone from Evolsdog. I know them all."

The girl came over and held Kat's hand. The child's smooth skin and small fingers felt strange in her palm, the gnarled hand of an old woman. Kat's other hand had moved to her throat and was fondling her necklace like an amulet to calm her thumping heart. Belatedly she realized its shape. She held it up and saw the crystal acorn. Saw the gold cube at its center and dropped it, startled.

"What's the matter, Grandma?"

"How did I get this? Where did—"

"Grandpa," said Kitty. "Before he died. He had it made for you. It was an anniversary gift. Because of your story."

"My story?" said Kat.

"When you fell from that tree."

"But that... was years ago."

"During your birthday party. When you were nine."

"Of course, yes," said Kat. It was beginning to come back to her. She smiled at her granddaughter. She brought Kitty's hand up to kiss her fingers affectionately. "I'm forgetful. Remind me again."

Kitty sat beside her where Kat had patted the bed.

"Which part, Grandma?"

"I was a bit of a daredevil, wasn't I?"

"You were. You climbed that tree on a dare. You went all the way out on a limb to—"

"Reach a nest of eggs."

"And you made it," said Kitty.

"Except there was an earthquake. Wasn't there?"

"And you fell. You almost died. You *did* die."

Kat blinked, wincing. "My heart. It stopped. I was told."

Kitty nodded. "Only for a few minutes."

"It felt longer." Kat smiled and gazed into her granddaughter's eyes, eggshell blue, same as hers. "Like our dreams. Like days."

"But you came back and lived. Isn't that amazing?"

"Yes, amazing," said Kat. "A moment ago, I thought..."

"What did you think, Grandma?"

"That I was staring into a three-dimensional mirror and seeing myself inside it. That you were me. Isn't that crazy?"

"No," said Kitty, hugging Kat. "We *are* alike. I want to be just like you. I *am* like you. I wish you could have seen me. I climbed to the top of an oak tree today. Just for you."

"For me? Why?"

"Someday I'm going to travel to Evolsdog too."

Kat had a sudden glimpse of the cobblestone streets and village beyond the four walls. "You will, Kitty. When it's your time."

"But I want to go there *now*, Grandma."

"No." Kat tightened the grip to her granddaughter's hands and felt her own youth passing through her again, which made her smile. "This is now. Enjoy life to its fullest while you are *here*."

"Love being here now," said Kitty.

"That's right," said Kat.

"Said Wyatt T. Frog." Kitty made a face, widening her eyes.

It made Kat laugh. "I do approve, even encourage you to climb those trees. Just be careful. Remember. Fear *is* your friend."

"Warned Riley Crow."

"Who kept insisting he came along *only* to keep me safe."

"What a liar." Kitty smirked. "Don't worry, Grandma. I won't do anything stupid. At least for another day or two. I promise."

Kat smiled.

"I *am* getting good grades. Except I do visit the principal's office every now and then. Just for fun. Every cog has to fit to function.

Right? Which, I guess, means cognition too?"

"You're smart. That one took me awhile longer to get."

"I love you, Grandma."

Kat was stroking her acorn pendant, belatedly realizing that she was, and held it up to the light to see the gold cube inside. "I want you to know I'm leaving this for you, Kitty. After I'm—"

"*Grandma.*"

"I didn't mean *today*," laughed Kat. "Let's hope not."

Kitty laughed too, uneasily.

"It's all right." Kat rubbed her granddaughter's hand between her thumb and fingers, calming them both. She became disoriented for a moment, then smiled. "I was happy. I had a pretty good life here, didn't I?"

"You had an amazing life, Grandma. You're famous."

Kat was puzzled. "For what?"

"Grandma. Your stories about Evolsdog."

Kat was blindly touching her face, her fingertips moving along the deep wrinkles, as if the lines could trace back to her memories, to who she was. She lifted the mirror to see herself again.

"How did this happen?"

"What, Grandma?"

Kat looked away from the oval glass, this reflective pool frozen in its frame, this portal, and gave a curious laugh.

"What is it, Grandma?"

"When did I get to be so old? I swear, if it wasn't for this face in the mirror, I would think I was still a young girl, like you."

"But then you wouldn't be my grandma."

"How true. It is best this way. How old are you now?"

"I turned *nine*. Today! Can you believe it?"

"Like me, as I was. Happy birthday. Where is everyone?"

"Cleaning up after my party. I'll go tell mom you're awake."

"No, wait," said Kat. "Stay with me awhile longer."

Kitty sat back on the bed. "This is so strange."

"Strange how?"

"I was praying, just now, hoping you would wake so we could talk like we used to. For 'hours on end' like you used to say to me. And suddenly you awoke. On my *ninth* birthday."

"Yes. That is strange," said Kat.

"But it's not a coincidence."

"No," said Kat. "There are no coincidences here."

Kitty grinned. "Said the praying mantis."

Kat smiled. "Yes, he did."

"I'm really glad you're awake, Grandma."

Kat laughed, patting her hand. "I too am glad, Kitty. But it does beg the question: Where *exactly* are we?"

"Mom and Dad arranged to bring you home for my birthday. That was my birthday wish. For you to be here."

"Thank you."

"For what?"

"Bringing me home."

Kat pushed aside the mirror. She took her granddaughter's hand and clutched it in her hands. She then closed her eyes and smiled. It was a look of satisfaction.

"May I ask for a wish? Even though this is your special day?"

"Anything, Grandma."

"I would love to hear you tell me. In your words."

"Tell you what?"

"My story."

"Your story?"

"Who I was."

Made in the USA
Monee, IL
07 July 2026

56552169R00134